To Love You More

WAYNE JORDAN

KIMANI™
ROMANCE

To my readers who continue to give
their unwavering support. You are the reason I write.

To Jayne, Danica and the other beautiful "hosties"
of the Harlequin Community who share, with me,
a love for reading.

KIMANI PRESS™

ISBN-13: 978-0-373-86255-9

TO LOVE YOU MORE

Recycling programs
for this product may
not exist in your area.

Dear Reader,

I hope you enjoy *To Love You More,* a story of second chances. *To Love You More* represents my growth as a published author. I can't believe that five years have passed! I took a long time to write this book, but I wanted it to be perfect, and as I write *The End,* I know that it's the best love story I've written.

I hope you, my readers, enjoy George and Rachel's story. It's what you've come to expect from a Wayne Jordan story—an exotic, tropical setting and an intense, passionate love story. Of course, George is the kind of hero my female fans love. Sexy, arrogant and, in this case, a mass of rippling muscles.

I've already started work on a new series about sisters and the rugged, handsome men who'll sweep them off their feet.

Be sure to visit me at my website, www.waynejordan.net, or email me at authorwj@caribsurf.com.

May God continue to bless you.

Until…

Wayne Jordan

Chapter 1

"How'd you like to go to the movies with me?" The deep, husky voice sent shivers down her spine.

Rachel Davis looked up from the book she was reading. She frowned. It was George Simpson…a boy in her class.

His eyes caressed her boldly, making her breathless and uncomfortable. She didn't like him much, found him arrogant and brash, but her body betrayed her each time he looked in her direction.

He was good on the eyes, a bit on the short side, but what he lost in his height, he made up for in a well-toned physique. She had heard he'd recently won the local bodybuilding competition for school boys and she could see why—the rippling muscles did make him blatantly sexy.

She didn't know him well, had only smiled at him

on a few occasions, but she realized he couldn't keep his eyes off her.

She scowled. She had no plans of being the source of locker room boasting. Did he really think she was stupid enough to go out with him? She'd only enrolled at the school a few weeks ago, but already she'd heard enough stories about him to be wary.

"One of your girlfriends busy?" she asked, her voice laced with sarcasm. She didn't look up, hoping he'd get the message and go away.

"I'd give them all up just for a date with you," he replied smoothly, an unexpected sincerity in his voice.

"It doesn't say much about what you think of your relationships," she responded. This time she raised her head, looking him straight in the eyes. *Beautiful, pale brown eyes.*

"Relationships? I just have friends," he replied cheerfully. "With you, I'd want a relationship." His eyes twinkled.

"I'm sorry, I don't have time for relationships or a smooth-talking spoiled brat who feels he has to get into every girl's panties."

He cringed. She could tell she'd shocked him.

But then he grinned, a sardonic tilt of his lips.

"While the image of the panties may be stimulating, I'm going to prove to you that I can change. That player, he's not the real me and I'm willing to put him to rest," he responded, reaching a hand out to touch hers.

She jerked her hand away. "Well, I can promise you that you won't have an easy task ahead of you. I'm immune to *boys* like you."

He raised a single brow, the emphasis on her use of *boys* not lost.

"I'm fine with that. When the prize is going out with the woman I plan to marry someday, no task can be too difficult."

She snorted in disgust, an unladylike sound that made her squirm. He really was full of himself. Why did he think that any sensible girl would fall for his crap?

"While I'm enjoying the conversation," she said, her voice oozing with sarcasm, "I do have a test in an hour and need to study. Some of us are not as naturally gifted as you are."

At her comment, he stared at her sharply. With a final nod of his head, he turned and walked away.

Rachel watched his retreat. He was good-looking, more than good-looking.

And she was attracted to him, had been from the first time he'd walked, no, strutted, into the classroom, clothed in his air of importance.

It had been her first day at The Lodge School. She'd hated that her parents had wanted her to switch high schools, but she couldn't help but agree that she needed more of an academic challenge, and The Lodge School was the perfect place.

A school with a tradition of excellence didn't come close to describing one of Barbados's best. Her father had attended Lodge many years before, so the school had been the ideal choice. Already she loved it here and had finally admitted that her father had made a fine decision.

From her early teens, she had dreamed of being a lawyer, and coming here was a step in the right direction if she wanted to achieve that dream.

Then she'd seen *him*. She could tell that he worked out…and often. Even at sixteen, or maybe seventeen, he was well-toned with broad shoulders, a neat waist and arms that seemed as if they would burst through the white cotton shirt that was part of the school uniform. The gray trousers he wore hung loosely but did little to hide his muscular thighs.

That first day, he'd swaggered into the classroom and the eyes of every girl, and some of the boys, had devoured him.

He greeted them all with a "What's up?" and headed to the front of the classroom, where he chatted with two equally handsome boys—Troy Whitehall and Shayne Knight. Later, she would discover they were the best of friends and, when not at classes, inseparable.

And then she realized that each time she looked in his direction, he'd be staring at her, that sexy, knowing smile on his face. But he never approached her, as if biding his time, as if waiting for the perfect moment to pounce.

Well, he'd finally made his move and if his reaction to her rejection was anything to go by, he'd probably not want to say anything to her again.

She watched his retreating back and noticed that, despite her rejection, he still walked with an air of confidence.

No, he wasn't one to give up.

Before he turned the corner, he stopped and looked back. And then he flashed that tantalizing grin that lit his face up and made him look oh so sexy.

In that moment, Rachel knew that if he didn't give up, he was going to win. Already, her indifference to him was melting slowly away.

George could tell Rachel liked him. She might have appeared indifferent, but he could tell that she was attracted. From the day he'd walked into the classroom and seen her, he had fallen under her magical spell.

He found himself spending most of his class time staring at her. Fortunately, he had a quick mind and could pick up the work they'd done during the day. He tried to avoid doing it too much but inevitably his eyes would stray in her direction.

One of the plusses was that she was in all of his classes and, though he had no idea what he wanted to do after graduation, a career in law was looking like the ideal choice. His decision had been partially influenced by her own revelation during a recent Social Studies class.

He'd floated some possibilities around, but when Rachel had announced that she would be studying law, he'd echoed her choice when he made his own presentation. He'd noticed her reaction.

He had no doubt that he'd get into law school. Of the students in his class, he or one of his two best friends would finish at the top. Troy held the position most of the time, but he could tell that Rachel would challenge them for the top spot. It was not going to be easy for any of them to maintain supremacy. She rattled off facts in class that left him wondering if he was dumb.

He couldn't understand why Rachel was affecting him in this way. He liked girls, enjoyed being with them and despite what everyone said, he still had his virginity intact, a decision he'd made in his early teens. While his hormones raged and he often came close to giving in to his teenage need to do it, he remembered what his mother always said. "There ain't no rush, boy. Take ya time."

But this new girl was different. There was something

about her that fascinated him and made him want to make love to her. Nights were worse. He'd find himself awake and thinking about her…into the early hours of the morning.

He loved the way she wore her hair—in a short afro that made her so cute, if a bit boyish, but there was nothing boyish about her body. She was filling out in all the right places.

She was tall and slim, just under six feet and a bit taller than he was, but that didn't matter. In his early teens, he'd been a bit worried about his height, but the girls didn't seem to care.

He made love to them by perfecting the art of foreplay. When he dropped them home after a few hours of intense passion, he'd leave them drained and satiated; he didn't think they even realized they'd not gone all the way.

He'd always been amazed at what he could do with his hands and mouth and tongue that would leave them totally happy.

For him, there was no time that a woman's mouth on him couldn't take him to heaven and back.

But recently, none of those girls were on his mind.

Rachel consumed his every waking hour. At breakfast, he'd think about her, on his way to and from school, but it was in the early hours of the morning, when he'd wake, hot and horny, from dreaming about her, her scent somehow lingering. He'd occasionally have to take things in hand, but that was only a temporary solution to the need that consumed him.

He knew as sure as the sun would rise each day that they would eventually make love.

That evening as he sat in the school's cricket pavilion, celebrating the team's victory against a longtime rival, he couldn't help thinking about her.

"You're very quiet, George. You in love or what?" Troy teased.

He didn't answer. He wasn't even sure what was going on.

"Now, I said that as a joke, but you didn't answer, so something must be wrong."

George turned to Troy, hoping that his eyes did not reveal the warring emotions.

"It's that new girl?" Troy asked. "What's her name?"

"Rachel," he said without hesitation.

"What's going on, George?" He could hear the genuine concern in his friend's voice.

"Nothing. Everything. Man, I'm not even sure," he grumbled, tossing the cricket ball to the ground in frustration.

"I would not have believed you'd be the first to fall. Shayne is more that kind of guy. I always predicted that he'd be the first to get serious. Then me. But you?"

"Troy, you know me better than that," he responded.

"I do. I *thought* I knew you, but all of a sudden you've gone crazy for the girls. You better be using condoms. I thought we vowed we'd never let anything get in the way of our dreams. You…a lawyer. Me…a doctor and Shayne… Well, he isn't quite sure yet, but I know it'll more likely be engineering or architecture. He hasn't made up his mind. Of course, his parents would prefer him to do agriculture. They want him to take over the plantation."

"Is that the impression you have of me?" he asked. "I ain't been having sex."

"So why is everyone thinking you're scoring with all those girls?" Troy admonished.

"It's just a mind thing," George reasoned. "I've been scoring, but not in the way everyone seems to think. I know we made that vow and I have no intentions of breaking it. My dreams come first."

"You're trying to tell me that you're still a virgin?"

"Shush." George put a finger to his lips. "No need to tell the world about my status."

"I promise," Troy said, laughing loudly. "It's between you and me. So you're the only one of us who's still pure? So ironic. Most people would think the opposite."

"And isn't that a good thing?" he asked, rising from where he was sitting.

"Why? I know you feel a bit off center because of your height. But with all the girls running after you, you shouldn't be too worried. And as far as I'm concerned, five-six isn't short. What you lose in height, you've made up for with those muscles. All the girls at school are drooling over you."

"They are, aren't they?" he replied, his chest puffed up. He strutted across the bleachers, stopping to pose, flaunting his rippling muscles.

"No need to get all conceited on me," Troy said. "Why don't you use some reverse psychology? I'm sure Rachel is enjoying the attention. Just ignore her for a few days and I bet she will eventually come to you."

"I'm not sure if it's going to be easy to ignore her. Man, a girl has never done this to me before. I can't understand what's happening to me." He lowered himself to the bench.

"You're in love," Troy stated calmly, his hand resting on George's shoulder.

"L-love," he stammered. "I'm not in love. I don't even know what love is."

"Well, you're discovering. I'm glad I'm not like you. I'm not even going to encourage that. I hang with a girl every once in a while, get what I want and move on. No emotional attachment. My schoolwork comes first."

"Your books always come first," George remarked. "But it's not about you. It's about your father and what he wants. I keep telling you that you have to live your own life. Not for your father."

"While it may be a bit about my father, I want to be a doctor. Not because my father is one but because I want to be," Troy said firmly.

"Well, I'm glad I don't have a father breathing down my neck all the time."

"I know you better than that, George. Saying it is not going to make it true."

George did not respond. Instead, he stood. "Come on, man, let's go. Everyone's already left. You want to come over for dinner? You know my mother always has a plate for you."

"Call Shayne and find out if he wants to come over too."

"He went to Tamara's dance recital, remember?"

They laughed, the sound echoing across the cricket pitch.

"I can just imagine him right now. He must be dying with embarrassment. I'm so glad I'm an only child...no sister to invite me to her dance recitals," Troy said. He stood and executed a clumsy pirouette.

More laughter.

"Better him than me," Troy continued. "Tamara invited me, but I was so glad I could tell her we had a cricket match. I know Shayne is sorry he didn't play for the team this season."

"Yes, he must be regretting it. Come on, I'll call Mom and let her know we're on our way."

"Cool, I'll call mine and let her know I'll be at your house. You can help me with the calculus homework."

Rachel yawned. She was tired. She glanced at the clock on the wall above her desk. Just after midnight. She'd not planned on studying so late. She needed to get a good night's sleep since she had an important test tomorrow. She was ready for it.

She sighed. Her studies had been her focus from the time her parents had discovered that she was gifted. Academics came easy for her. She didn't need to study long hours, even though she did anyway. She always wondered why her friends considered studying a chore. She only had to read something once and its essence would be imprinted on her mind.

She never boasted about her ability. She just accepted it for what it was—a talent she had. It was that and no more. The As were okay, but it was the knowledge she was gaining that was important. She wanted to be a lawyer. Hard work was the only way she would succeed.

But her focus was changing. She found herself thinking about George more and more. She'd been attracted to boys in the past, but there was something dangerous and exciting about him. He exuded a confidence and maturity that stirred her budding womanhood. In fact, compared to the two other boys he hanged with, he seemed the most mature, the most experienced.

He had this way of walking that made her think of doing things she'd never done before. She'd always wondered why good girls found some bad boys attractive. She now knew why. She'd heard the talk about him. He was definitely bad.

She ached to run her hand along the muscles that bulged under his school shirts. She wanted him to kiss her.

Rachel snorted in disgust. She'd be studying and then she'd start thinking about him and her body would ache all over with her need, the way it was doing now.

In that moment, she realized something. She was falling in love with him!

She didn't want that to happen. She knew what happened when girls fell in love. They would lose focus and their schoolwork would suffer.

She was seventeen years old and she had one more year in the sixth form. Then, it would be college and finally law school. At least five years of study before she became a practicing attorney.

And that was what should be the focus of her life. Not some romantic fantasy about the bad boy in her class.

She glanced around her room. It was a typical teenage girl's haven. For the past few years she'd planned on having it redecorated, but each year would pass by and she'd do nothing. But she had realized something recently. She was a woman now and it scared her. She'd been so wrapped up in her childhood, she had not paid attention to the changes happening within her.

George had forced her from her comfort zone to recognize her budding sexuality. She'd never had a boyfriend. The other girls in her class constantly boasted about their sexual exploits. She'd been shocked at many of their revelations, wondering what their parents would think if they only knew the truth about their sweet little girls.

She closed the history book. The Haitian Revolution had lost its appeal. She'd go to bed. That's what she needed to do.

She rose from sitting at her desk and slipped off her clothes, sliding naked between the sheets on her bed. She loved to sleep that way, the sheet's silky softness caressing her, its effect pleasant against her skin.

She closed her eyes, but the image of George remained bold and clear. When she fell asleep her dreams were of him as he lay next to her, his own body naked.

The rest of the semester passed without event. Over time, George's charm slowly melted Rachel's resistance. She admired his persistence. Maybe she shouldn't call it persistence. He didn't ignore her, neither did he make her feel pressured. He spoke to her when they came into contact, nothing more. But at times, she would notice his hungry gaze on her when he thought she wasn't looking.

On the day she turned eighteen, a basket of flowers arrived at her home. The card read: With Love—G. The script was bold and strong like he was. There was arrogance in the stroke of each letter.

He knew he didn't need to say anything more. The knowledge that he'd sent the flowers had left her feeling flustered and frustrated. She had vowed to resist him, but she knew now that her surrender was inevitable. The temptation was too appealing. There was so much about him she liked and admired.

More and more, she'd found herself responding to his body. He would pass by her, so close, and he'd smile slyly, reveling in the way she stiffened in reaction to him. For the rest of the day, the woodsy scent of his cologne would linger.

The night after her birthday, while she sat doing her homework, the doorbell rang. She groaned. Her parents were out and she didn't want to get up. The doorbell went again. She stood, annoyed at being disturbed from her studying, and headed downstairs. It could be someone important. When she reached the landing, she walked toward the door, pulling the curtains apart to check who was there.

Her heart stopped. George. What was he doing here?

She balked, glancing down at the clothes she wore. She should have looked in the mirror before she came downstairs.

Her heart racing, she stifled the urge to rush back upstairs. She unlocked the door, pulling it open.

"What can I do for you?" she asked, trying to sound unaffected by his appearance.

"It's your birthday," he replied, as if that answer was enough.

"I'm quite aware that yesterday was my birthday."

"Did you get my flowers?" he asked.

"Yes," she replied, softly. His gesture had been so romantic. Already, her anger at him—because he'd ruffled her, interrupted her, managed to get her attention—had abated.

"Aren't you going to ask me in?" he finally said.

"My parents are not at home. I'm not allowed to have anyone here when they're not."

"That's fine. Can you come out, so I can talk with you?"

She hesitated, and then stepped outside.

"I wanted to have an important chat with you," he said.

She shrugged.

"You know that I like you."

She nodded slowly.

"And I think you like me even though you pretend

not to. So I'd like to invite you out on a date—if your parents will approve. I want to say up front that my intentions are noble. I know you hear stuff about me. Some true, some far from the truth."

"You do have a reputation," she stated.

"I know, but most of those rumors are false."

She didn't respond, only stared at him with skeptical eyes.

"Okay, I'll go out with you," she said eventually.

The look of surprise on his face made her smile.

"Everyone needs a chance," she responded. "This is your first and last one."

"So how about Saturday?" he asked. "We can go to the cinema and then out to eat. That's fine with you? I want to treat you for your birthday."

"Sounds good."

He continued to smile.

"Well, have a good night," he said.

"I will," she replied. "Thanks for inviting me out."

He nodded and waited until she closed the door, then moved off. She peered through the curtains as he walked down the pathway.

When he reached his car, he turned back and waved at her before driving away.

It was only then that Rachel realized her knees had been shaking.

Their first date was magical. The coolness of the night contrasted with the heat coursing through her body. Everything had been perfect.

Just before midnight, they walked slowly to her house, her hand in his. She wished the night would not end.

Just before the verandah, under the canopy of the

massive mahogany tree, he pulled her into his arms and held her close. She rested her head against his chest, feeling the rapid beat of his heart. He touched her chin, asking her to look up.

When she did, he lowered his head, capturing her lips with his.

She'd expected fireworks, but instead she heard soft music.

His tongue slipped between her lips, stirring the un-tapped heat deep inside her.

She could taste him, the minty tang of the dinner mint that still lingered.

Eventually, he pulled away, leaving her breathless and aching for more.

He smiled down at her.

"Wow," he said. "Just as I expected."

"Thanks for taking me out. I enjoyed the evening."

"I did too," he replied. "Want to do it again?"

"I'd love to. Just let me know when. I'll see you at school tomorrow."

"I can hang with you at school?"

"I'd like that."

He lowered his head again, his lips brushing hers lightly. "Sweet dreams, honey," he whispered.

He turned reluctantly. She didn't want him to go. She watched as he walked toward his car.

She was in love. She'd fallen in love with the school's notorious playboy.

Rachel slipped her jeans off, all the while feeling his gaze linger on her. She shivered. She felt uncomfort-able. She'd never done this before.

They'd been dating for four weeks now, but she felt

as if she'd known him forever. She was totally in love and her desire for him intensified until she had begged him to make love to her.

Strong arms wrapped around her from behind, offering comfort. He was incredibly gentle and, immediately, her reservation about what she was doing dissipated.

She loved him and for now, that was all that mattered.

"I love you," George whispered in her ear. The gentle breath on her ear tickled and she laughed softly.

In the curve of her behind, she felt his hardness, his penis taut and firm against her.

His arousal excited her and she ached to turn and look at him, but he continued to rain kisses on her back until his mouth reached the curve of her waist, and he held her, turning her to face him.

He rose, his lips descending on hers and igniting her internal heat.

Her legs buckled, but he held her tenderly before she fell.

He lifted her up easily, his muscles hard beneath her hands.

He walked over to the bed, resting her gently on it before he joined her. His mouth trailed all over her body until it reached the core of her femininity. When his tongue slipped between the delicate folds, she experienced a sensation she'd never experienced before. Pure liquid heat coursed through her body until she felt as if she'd caught on fire. But this heat was different. It gave pleasure and settled between her legs, leaving her aching and begging for more.

When she stiffened and she stifled the unexpected scream, her body seemed as if in limbo. And then it happened. She trembled, and wave after wave of pleasure washed over her as she convulsed with the intensity of her first orgasm.

George moved from between her legs, rising above her and resting his torso against hers.

He shifted on her, spreading her legs slightly apart, before he looked down at her, her expression one of total wonder.

He reached for the pants on the ground, pulling something from one of the pockets…a condom.

She sighed in relief. She'd hoped he had one. She didn't want to get pregnant. She had her whole future ahead of her, but she wasn't sure she'd be able to stop him if he didn't have one. She wanted him so much.

She watched as he stood before her, his penis erect and firm. There was something wonderful about his appendage. It was monstrous. Large, with thick veins running through it. Apprehension made her hesitate for a moment.

She noticed him staring at her.

He smiled, as if he knew what she was thinking and was reassuring her.

She smiled in return, letting him know that she was fine, that she was ready for him. She felt better. She knew things would be all right.

"I want you now," she groaned. "I want to feel you inside me." She sounded bold and brazen, and that was exactly how she felt.

She wanted him and the anticipation of her first encounter was unbearable.

He settled gently on top of her, his hardness pressed against her womanhood. She ached to feel him inside her.

She felt a gentle probing at the entrance to her vagina

and she shifted her legs wider to give him easy access. He slipped slowly inside her until she could feel every long, thick inch of him. There was a moment of intense pain, but she wrapped her legs around his firm buttocks, locking him into her. The pain slowly abated, until all she could think of was the heat and hardness of his penis throbbing inside her.

For a while he did not move, but then he eased out and then in again, a sweet, powerful movement that sent fire coursing through her body.

He continued to stroke her, until she moaned and groaned with the joy she was experiencing.

And then she joined him, her own torso keeping the rhythm, his moans adding to the excitement of their coupling.

Deep inside her, the heat intensified until she felt she could bear it no more and release came in a shower of fiery rain washing over her with its power. Her body shuddered and contracted with the power of her orgasm.

In response, George's body tensed and he cried out loudly, his own release evident in the erratic jerking of his body, but he continued to stroke her long and hard, with a power that made the sweet rush overcome her again.

When he collapsed on top of her, his breathing heavy and erratic, she wrapped her arms around him and held him tightly. His lips found hers and he kissed her with a desperation that stirred the excitement inside her.

She wanted him again, but she knew enough about the male anatomy to know it would be a while.

He ended the kiss, his lips brushing her eyelids and nibbling her nose.

She giggled and he laughed in response.

Their eyes locked.

"I love you," he whispered.

"I love you too," she echoed, rubbing her body against him seductively.

She felt his penis stir. Maybe she was wrong.

"Make love to me again," she purred. "I need you inside me."

He smiled. "I'm happy to oblige. Anything to please my woman."

Chapter 2

Their lovemaking was different. It was hard to explain, but despite their desire for each other, Rachel now felt an unfamiliar distance between her and George. They'd been lovers for almost five years, and each time she had returned home to Barbados from England for holidays, their time together had always been special. At those times, she'd realize how much she loved him and how much he loved her.

Of that she was still sure, but there was something different. It wasn't another woman. At least, she didn't think so. If something was wrong, it had to be something else. As they'd made love, she'd felt the same kind of passion flowing from him. His lovemaking had been desperate, almost as if it would be the last time. A feeling of dread washed over her.

Immediately, she stifled the thought. She was being paranoid. Maybe not coming home for a whole year had not been a good thing. During the first four years of her studies in England, she came home each break—at Christmas and during the summer.

When her father had passed away last summer, she'd almost decided not to return to England. His death had devastated her. However, George had convinced her that her father would have wanted her to finish her studies, to fulfill her dream. She'd left the island reluctantly, knowing that she'd be gone for a full year but inspired by the fact that it was her final year.

Her studies finally behind her, Rachel had been admitted to the local bar and was ready to face the challenge of being a prosecutor. George had opted to remain in Barbados to earn his law degree and had just completed his final two years of law school in Trinidad. He'd wanted her to do the same thing, but her being awarded the scholarship to England had altered their plans. Her parents had insisted that she could not pass up the opportunity to study at Oxford University.

She'd relented after George had echoed her parents' sentiments, but being away from him had not been easy for either of them.

The past two weeks back home had been great, except for the niggling feeling that she'd tried so hard to ignore. The tiny engagement ring he'd given her, just before she left for England, felt heavy on her finger.

She sighed. Maybe she was just being paranoid.

Even now, looking down at a sleeping George made her heart ache with her love for him.

She slipped out of bed. She needed to take a shower and head out to work.

* * *

When she stepped out of the bathroom a half an hour later, George was no longer in bed. She dressed quickly and then headed to his study where he was probably already working.

At the entrance to the office, she stopped on hearing her name. He was talking about her.

"Troy, you know I love Rachel, but I'm no longer sure if I'm ready for marriage right now. I don't want anything to distract me from my goals and she's a definite distraction. I've been offered that fellowship. I want to go but I don't know what to tell her. She's going to be totally devastated. When she left to go to England I wanted nothing more in life than to marry her. I'm not sure if that's what I want anymore."

He paused for a moment before continuing, "But I don't know what to tell her."

There was silence again.

"Yes, I know I'm a man. I'll tell her. Maybe tonight. But I don't agree. She's not going to understand. Rachel may be a modern woman who wants to work, but deep inside she's still the marrying kind."

Rachel turned away from the study. She couldn't let him see her right now. The trickle of tears would let him know she'd overhead what he'd said. She'd go upstairs, wash her face and return downstairs. By then she'd be under control.

Upstairs, she washed her face and reapplied her makeup.

The door opened and he walked in.

She turned to him, searching his face for the evidence of his guilt, but he smiled back at her as if nothing was wrong. She smiled in response, fighting to control her anger.

"I have to go," she said. "I need to be at the office early this morning."

"No breakfast?" he asked.

"No, I really need to go." She could feel the onset of another wave of tears. "I'll call you when I get a chance."

"Cool. You're coming over tonight?" he asked.

"Yes, I'll be here."

"Okay," he replied, walking over to place a light kiss on her lips. "Make sure you get something to eat," he said.

"I'll do that," she replied. She picked up her handbag and waved goodbye.

Sitting in her car five minutes later, Rachel struggled to fight the tears threatening to fall. *I will not cry. I will not cry.*

"Marrying kind" indeed! She had always prided herself on being independent and an advocate for women's equality.

But what George had said was so close to the truth. She did want a husband, a good home and a family. She didn't see why she couldn't have all of it.

By the time she pulled into the parking lot of the judicial building, she'd mustered a modicum of calmness.

When she reached her office, a cup of steaming cappuccino in her hands, she'd pushed the events of the morning to the back of her mind. She needed to focus on her work. Tonight, she would worry about what she should say to George.

Something was definitely wrong. From the time she'd arrived at his apartment, he had sensed it. Rachel was unusually quiet. Not that she was the talkative type, but she seemed troubled by something.

She was probably worried about her first case.

He glanced furtively at her from the papers he was working on. He wanted to make love to her, but the guilt only made him feel worse.

He needed to talk to her, but with her pensiveness, he did not know if the right time was tonight. Yet, he knew he could not keep putting it off.

She lay on the sofa in his office. She appeared relaxed, but as he looked closer, he realized that there was a subtle tension in her body he hadn't noticed before.

He closed his papers. He needed to find out what was wrong.

When he reached the sofa, she looked up, a ready smile on her face, but a smile that didn't reach her eyes.

He lowered himself to the sofa, wanting to touch her but knowing that it would be better not to.

"You're ready to tell me what's wrong?" he finally asked.

"As if you don't know," she retorted unexpectedly.

Still confused, he shrugged his shoulders.

"How am I expected to know what's on your mind?"

She laughed, a sarcastic, guttural sound. "And I'm expected to know what's on yours?"

He reached out a hand to touch her, to calm the beast warring inside her.

"Don't touch me," she snapped.

He pulled back sharply, her words like a slap across his face.

"Now, this is getting a bit weird." He had never seen her in a mood like this.

"I heard your conversation with Troy this morning," she responded, her tone chilling the room.

He didn't know what to say. He wished the floor would open beneath him. But he realized that what would take place was inevitable. He'd wanted to talk with her, break his news quietly, gently.

"I'm sorry you had to hear it that way. I didn't mean to hurt you," he said gently.

"I thought you loved me. Thought we would spend the rest of our lives together," she pleaded. He could see the pain in her eyes.

"I do love you, Rachel. I'm just not ready for marriage. I have so much I want to do before I commit myself to a lifetime with you."

"You could have told me. I'm willing to wait."

"But I won't do that to you. I *can't* do that to you. I'm going to be studying for another two years and I'm not sure what's going to happen after that."

"You know what? You, Shayne and Troy are so alike. It's always about the dream—what *you* want to achieve in life at the expense of everything else."

She rose from the sofa. The look she tossed him was one of absolute disdain. The room suddenly turned chilly.

"Well, I think I should say goodbye now. I can see that I'm not wanted."

"Rachel, I don't want you to leave here angry at me."

"What did you expect, George?" she retorted. "That I would be all happy and smiling? Give me credit for being human. But I promise you, in a few days I'll be fine and you can get on with your life and your dreams. I'm strong and definitely a modern woman. I may be the 'marrying kind' as you said, but I assure you, I can survive without a man in my life."

She picked her bag up and slipped her feet into her shoes. With as much grace as she could muster, she walked out of the room without another word. The next noise he heard was the slamming of his front door.

Hours later, he still sat there, his heart still heavy with the magnitude of what he had done.

Rachel bent over the sink in the bathroom. For the second morning running she was not feeling well. She'd gone to the doctor after work that evening, but she didn't need a doctor to tell her what was wrong. *She was pregnant.* She had only needed the doctor to confirm it, but she knew there was a child growing insider her womb.

George's child.

She shook her head slowly. How on earth had this happened? They had always been careful to use protection.

In the past two months she'd seen him on occasion, but last week he had headed off to Australia for the fellowship. He'd tried to talk to her, but she had refused. She'd thought it best that the contact between them should end.

She had no idea what she was going to do. Letting George know was out of the question. She didn't want him to feel obliged to return home. He'd made it clear he wanted to go, that his career and dreams were more important.

She wished she had someone to talk to but her cadre of female friends didn't exist. She wondered if she could talk to Shayne or Troy, but that would be like telling

George directly. There was no way they would not tell him. So she was on her own.

An abortion was out of the question. She was definitely pro-life and had always made her position clear about her belief.

Already she loved the life growing inside her.

She wondered if it would be a girl or boy. She smiled, resting her hand against the warmth of her stomach.

The image of a tiny, squalling boy flashed in her mind. The baby would be a boy. She sensed it in the way only a pregnant mother could.

Her son would be all right. She would be all right. She was convinced of that.

She walked out of her room and down the corridor to her mother's room. She'd start by letting her mother know.

Later that week she stood at the window to her office, looking down at the empty courtyard. Though she'd stayed later than usual, she seemed unable to focus on the case she'd been working on.

There was a knock on her door.

Her boss, Edward St. Clair, stepped into the office.

Rachel turned from the window. She tried to look brave, but the weight of her pregnancy gave rise to another bout of tears. She was embarrassed. She was not one for crying, but she could not stop the constant flow.

"What's wrong, Rachel?" he asked anxiously. "I haven't even given you the bad news and you're crying already."

When she didn't respond, his expression became one of concern.

"What's wrong, Rachel?"

"I'm pregnant," she responded this time. There was no need to ramble all over the place.

"And you're crying? I would have thought you'd be happy."

"I am, but…" she mumbled.

"So there's a but?"

"Yes."

"George?" he asked.

"Yes, George."

"He's not happy?" he queried.

"He doesn't know. We broke up before he left."

"You did? I was expecting wedding bells sometime in the not so distant future."

"No, his future and his career are more important," she replied sarcastically.

She stopped. She'd told him a bit too much. It was really none of his business. He was her boss, nothing more.

"So you are planning on being a single mother?" he asked.

His words startled her. While she had thought about keeping the baby, she'd not thought about it in that light.

Single mother?

How was she going to raise a child alone?

"I'm sure that in a few months George will be getting phone calls from all his friends."

Another complication she had not thought about. George would eventually know. It was inevitable.

Edward smiled.

"I have the perfect solution to your problem," he said.

She raised her brow nonchalantly.

"I was about to tell you my bad news, but under the

circumstances, it could be good news. You just have to agree to my proposal."

"Proposal?" she asked warily.

"I was coming to let you know I've been offered a job in Anguilla. I applied a few months ago but, quite frankly, didn't expect to be offered the position."

"You're leaving?" She could not contain her disappointment.

"Marry me," he said.

At the expression of shock she knew was registered on her face, he raised his hand.

"I'm quite aware that I'm way older than you are. This is only a marriage of convenience. I need a wife. It will give respectability to my position. You need a father for your child. You may have to put your career on hold for a few years. Of course, I'll make no sexual demands on you."

There was silence.

"I don't know what to say," she finally said. His words had slowly started to sink in.

"Don't say anything now. Go home and think about it and tomorrow you can let me know your decision," he said.

She watched as he walked out of her office.

Maybe this was what she needed. Look what passion had done—left her young and pregnant.

She closed her eyes. It was times like these when she wished she had someone to talk to. She'd made no lasting friends at school. For years, she'd been a loner. She'd been focused on her studies...and on George.

There was one girl at school she'd been sort of

friends with, but after high school, the girl had disappeared and they'd lost contact.

The reality was that if she left the island, she'd lose nothing, no one would miss her. Not even Shayne or Troy. Because of her years studying overseas she'd never really gotten close to them, except for the few occasions they'd been out as a group, and even then she and George had been focused on each other.

Later that night, she picked the phone up and called her boss. She'd been about to put the phone down when he answered. That had sealed her fate.

"I'll go with you to Anguilla. I'll marry you, but under one condition."

"What's that?" he replied.

"That you promise to treat my child as your own—that you love him as your own. He is never to know that you're not his real dad."

"I can agree to that. My late wife and I never had any kids. So it'll be good to have someone to spoil."

"I still think you're being crazy, but your proposal is definitely a good solution to my situation. I'm not sure how my mom is going to deal with my leaving, but she will respect my decision. Would it be all right for her to come and visit us in Anguilla?"

"Definitely, your mother will always be welcome to visit. I have to go. I have an engagement to attend. We'll talk tomorrow. We have lots of planning and arranging to do."

"Thank you."

"I should be saying thank you."

With that he put the phone down.

Rachel sat there, her thoughts still troubled by what she was about to do.

* * *

George flung the glass against the wall. He still couldn't believe what he'd heard.

The bitch!

He could believe that she'd left the island. He couldn't believe that she had married Judge Edward St. Clair.

He picked up another glass, filled it with his favorite brandy and swallowed it down. A part of him felt like screaming and cussing, but another part of him just wanted to lie on the bed and cry. But he wouldn't! He wouldn't cry for her. She'd betrayed him in the cruelest way. Just three months after their breakup she was getting married and, to add insult to injury, to a man almost twice her age.

He set the glass down, glad that his room was a fair distance from his mother's room. He hoped she had not heard his rage.

He stripped his clothes off, stood naked and looked into the mirror. His old concern about his height threatened to surface, but what he saw in the mirror lay his crazy thoughts to bed.

He knew he looked good. His physique was superior and the girls loved his manhood. He tried to look at it critically, but what he saw pleased him. Maybe he was a bit too obsessed with his manhood, but he wasn't a bad person. He had changed. He'd made adjustments to his social life. Abstinence was his new motto, but what had it done for him?

She'd gone and married someone else.

But who did he have to blame but himself? He was the one to break their relationship off. He'd been the one to hurt her. She'd been the one to beg him not to end what they had.

So the only person he could blame was himself. He'd put himself in the situation.

He had not even heard about the wedding.

George had arrived back home from Australia for a holiday and he'd been greeted by the announcement in the newspaper. The judge had been offered a position in Anguilla and had gone with his new wife—Rachel.

The phone rang, startling him with its harsh volume. He walked over and glanced at the caller display. It was Troy. He'd expected it.

He picked the phone up and found himself unable to speak.

"It's Troy. I'm coming over."

He mumbled something he wasn't even sure of and listened for the inevitable click.

He lowered himself to the couch, the tears already trickling from his eyes. He tried to stem their flow but couldn't. When Troy entered his room thirty minutes later, he'd regained control.

He'd made a vow. Never again would he allow a woman to make him cry. As far as he was concerned, Rachel St. Clair no longer existed.

Chapter 3

Thirteen Years Later

The woman gliding toward him piqued his interest. A tall woman, she walked with the kind of grace that few women could achieve even after long hours of practice. She had her head down, browsing the pages of a folder she carried.

And then it struck him. There was something familiar about her.

Rachel.

What the hell was *she* doing in Barbados?

No, he had to be wrong. He was letting his imagination run wild.

He increased his stride, walking quickly along the corridor of the newly constructed courthouse.

When she turned the corner, he followed her. She was heading in the same direction he was.

And then she stopped and turned around. She must have heard his footsteps.

Time stopped and he saw the woman he'd once loved more than life itself.

White-hot anger burned him, but immediately he felt like laughing. The whole situation seemed a bit ridiculous.

He wasn't sure about her reaction, but the eyes that looked back at him now were dull, indifferent.

George tried to say something but wasn't sure what the right words would be.

She solved the problem by speaking first.

"George." She smiled briefly, very briefly.

"Rachel," he replied. "You're the last person I'd have expected to see this bright Monday morning."

"I returned to the island a few weeks ago. This is my first day in court."

"You're with a law firm?"

"No, I'm a prosecutor."

"Why am I not surprised? That's what you've always wanted to do."

"And need I ask? You did always make it clear you wanted a private practice."

"Yes, I'm a partner in a law firm."

"That's good. I always knew you would be successful," she responded. She glanced down at her watch. "It was nice seeing you, but I have to go. I don't like to be late getting into court."

"That's fine. I have to be going too. I'll be seeing you around."

Her expression told him that she didn't think seeing him was something to be thrilled about. And she was right. He didn't think seeing her was good for his equilibrium.

She nodded politely, turned and walked away, her stride purposeful. She didn't look back and he felt a pain so intense that he wondered how having her back in Barbados was going to affect him. If his current reaction was any indication, he still had strong feelings for her.

She was beautiful. In fact, she was more beautiful than she'd been those many years ago. In that short moment, he'd noticed so many things about her. She'd definitely changed. She was still tall and slender, but she'd filled out in all the right places. There was a maturity about her that made her more sophisticated—and sexier.

Her hair was longer. Back then she'd had trouble keeping the long curly mess from her face, so she had cut it into the cute, short afro he remembered. Now it was shoulder-length and the curls were gone.

He headed to the courtroom. She'd shaken him up and it took all of his willpower to regain his composure.

Five minutes later, when he stepped into the courtroom, the sight of Rachel sitting on the prosecutor's side stopped him in his tracks.

Damn, his day had suddenly gone from bad to worse. How on Earth was he going to do a good job with Rachel across the room from him?

And then he realized it would be easier than he thought. All he had to remember was that she had dumped him for a man almost twice his age.

He sighed heavily and stepped confidently into the room. All eyes turned in his direction, but he was staring at one pair of eyes, which, flashing angrily, stared back at him.

Rachel was as unhappy as he was!

An hour later, George exited the courtroom. Fiery anger surged through his veins. He'd never felt so embarrassed before. He couldn't believe he'd lost the case. He had not lost a single case since starting his own firm. His record of being an "arrogant son of a bitch" was in tatters. And the case wasn't a difficult one either. Not that his client would get any jail time, but the fine he would have to pay was more than they'd expected.

And all because of Rachel. He should have congratulated her afterward, but he'd been too shocked at his loss.

When she'd made her closing argument, she was calm and forceful, a ready smile on her face for the jury and judge. By the time she'd concluded, they had been eating out of her hands. She had been good, really good, he admitted grudgingly.

He'd been good too, but she'd been better.

Behind him, he heard the sharp clip of a woman's heels, and then her husky voice called his name.

"George, George."

He stopped. Didn't she see that he was not in the mood for talking to anyone? Especially her?

"What's wrong? You come to rub your victory in my face?"

She stopped suddenly, the look on her face one of literal pain. Immediately, he regretted his reaction.

"I can see it makes no sense trying to speak with

you on a professional level," she said, her voice cold. "I won't take any more of your time."

"I'm sorry," he replied, reaching out to touch her hand as she turned to walk away. The spark of awareness startled him.

She stopped, her body stiff with the tension. She turned slowly to look at him. Her expression was veiled. He could no longer tell what she was thinking. She'd recovered quickly.

"What can I do for you?" he asked, trying to remain as polite as possible.

"I've been away for a long time and just wanted to clear the air."

"Clear the air. What for?" he scoffed. "I'm cool with what you did. I'm over it."

"If that were so you wouldn't be acting as you are now," she reasoned.

"Maybe I'm just being human," he retorted.

"You were the one who broke up with me," she said. He couldn't understand how she could be so calm when his anger threatened to explode.

He paused for a moment. What she was saying was true, but he still felt as if she'd betrayed him.

"I know that," he finally said. "But it didn't take you long to get over me."

He looked at her and noticed a flash of uncertainty. But almost immediately the confident woman he'd seen in court was back.

He wasn't sure he liked this Rachel. She was different. The Rachel he'd grown up with had been warm and friendly. Yes, she had been quiet and introverted, but this woman in front of him was cold and distant.

Those were the words he'd use…cold and distant. She had loved to laugh and smile. This Rachel didn't smile much. He could tell.

"I will make things simple for you. We can let bygones be bygones. Neither of us is to blame for what happened. We were just two young kids who didn't know what we wanted out of life. We've survived the past thirteen years without each other. Maybe that's an indication that we didn't need each other."

"You're right," she replied, nodding, her face still expressionless.

"We are just two lawyers on opposite sides of the bench. We can maintain a good business relationship since it's inevitable that we'll meet. If you can live with that, I'm game."

"Good. I'm glad we could resolve this," she replied, smiling for the first time. "How are Troy and Shayne doing?"

"They're doing fine. Shayne is married to a wonderful woman, and Troy's wedding is just around the corner."

For a moment she went silent, and he noticed a glimpse of sadness in her eyes. "I hope I get to see them," she said.

"I'm sure you will. The island is small. I'm surprised I haven't heard before today that you were here. When did you get back?"

"I've been back for about two months now. But I've been keeping relatively quiet at home with my mom and hoping that I'd get the job I'd been looking for. I started in the Department of Prosecutors a few weeks ago." She glanced down at her watch. "I'm really sorry, but I have to go."

"Take care," he replied. He watched as she walked away, and instinctively, the sigh of relief rushed for his body.

This was definitely not going to be easy.

Rachel refused to look back, though her desire to do so almost overwhelmed her.

Physically, he'd not changed much. He was still as sexy as ever. He wasn't as tall as the average guy, but she'd always been fascinated by the ripple of muscles that packed themselves into his physique.

He'd always compensated for his height with the lethal sex appeal that had made her, and all of the girls in their class, ache to be his. When he'd chosen her, she could not believe it. But she had dealt with the situation rationally and logically.

As she was dealing with her situation right now. Her secret weighed heavily on her heart and she wondered again if she should tell him, but she balked at the possible consequences.

Later that evening, when her son burst into the living room where she sat reading, her confusion about what to do had not abated.

"Mom, I hit two sixes today in the cricket match. The coach says I have a lot of talent."

She smiled, trying not to show her trepidation. Her son had ended up loving cricket, just like his father did.

"I'm glad," she responded. The most important thing was that her son was happy. When Edward had passed away she'd been reluctant to return to Barbados, but her mother's pleading had finally convinced her to return home.

She was worried about George seeing his son. Gregory favored George. In fact, Gregory looked so much like a photo of his father as a teenager, she had no doubt that George would know the truth the first time he saw him. The resemblance was uncanny.

She was glad Gregory had settled into school so easily. She knew he missed his stepfather. When Edward had discovered that he was dying, he'd begged her to let him tell Gregory that he was not his father. Edward had not wanted to die with the lie. She'd relented. At that time, Gregory had accepted it without question. A few days after Edward's funeral he'd asked if his father was still alive. She told him the truth, anticipating further questions. There had been none.

She reached out a hand and pulled him onto the couch. He laughed as he landed on her lap.

"Love you," she said, putting her arms around him and placing a kiss on his cheek.

"Love you too, Mom," he replied. "So what are we having for dinner? I made sandwiches for Grandma and me when I got home from school, but she's not feeling well. She has a headache."

"I'll go and see her. Why didn't you call me at work and let me know?"

"She told me not to. She said it was only a slight headache."

"Okay, but next time let her know I told you to call. Have you finished your homework?"

"Yes, but I'm doing some extra studying. I have a project that's due next week. I want to do it now and get it out of the way."

"That's great. So what do you want me to cook?"

"Macaroni and cheese? Fried chicken?"

"Okay, since you've been so good, but no pie—it's too much."

"I work it off at cricket, so there's no need to worry. I'm fit."

"Okay, go work on your project. I'll call you when dinner is done."

She smiled as he raced out of the room. At times, she forgot that he was twelve years old, with the energy he had.

She turned and left the room, walking down the hallway until she reached her mother's room.

She knocked on the door, entering when her mother didn't respond.

Glancing at her mother only confirmed her concern. Her mother appeared fragile and lethargic. She had tried on several occasions to get her to the doctor, but then she'd seem all good and sprightly...until today. She wondered if it was depression, but her mother's occasional good moods would always negate those feelings.

"You all right, Mom?" she asked, reaching the bed. She sat on the edge of the bed, and placed her hand on her mother's forehead. No fever.

"I'm fine, Rachel. Just a little headache."

"I'm going to take you to the doctor tomorrow. These headaches are becoming more frequent. We need to find out if anything's wrong."

"Okay," her mother replied. She was surprised. Her mother always found excuses for her ailments.

"Good. Are you hungry? I'm going to get dinner started."

"Gregory made sandwiches, but yes, I'm a bit hungry."

"Okay, give me an hour or so. I'll send Gregory with a glass of juice. You took your medication?"

"I did."

"That's good. You just lie here and rest yourself. You'll be all right in a bit."

"I'm sure I will. I'm sorry I couldn't cook dinner."

"It's fine, Mom. I just want you to be well."

"Gregory finished his homework?" her mother asked.

"You know you don't have to ask that. He always does his homework."

"Yes, he's a good boy. Intelligent for his age. A bit too serious for my liking, but hopefully he'll lighten up now he and Marjorie's son are friends. Jonathan can talk nonstop. I'll bet he talks in his sleep."

"Gregory will be fine. Now, you rest yourself."

She bent and kissed her mother's forehead. When Grace closed her eyes, Rachel left and headed to her room, where she quickly took a shower and donned shorts and a T-shirt.

In the kitchen she prepared dinner, but she struggled to keep the images of George from her mind. He hadn't changed much and her response to him was a cause for concern. She didn't want to be attracted to him, but her body seemed to have a mind of its own.

He was just as handsome as he'd always been. Time had been good to him. With the exception of a few gray hairs at his temple, he didn't look a day older than when she'd left.

He was still muscular but not the bulging muscles like before. Instead, his body was lithe and made him seem taller than he actually was.

His height had never worried her back then. In fact,

she'd been glad to find someone who was not too tall. She didn't have to strain her neck looking up at him. The George she'd known had always been confident and a bit arrogant. That part of him had definitely not changed.

In court today, he'd exuded confidence and she'd admired the way he had handled the witnesses. She'd felt like a novice, but she'd had one up on him with her evidence so she had not been surprised at her win. She suspected that George had allowed his overconfidence to get in the way.

The look on his face, as the verdict had been read, said a lot. The next time they faced each other in court, she would not win so easily.

George watched the final moments of the game then turned the television off.

He rose from the sofa, glancing at the clock on the wall.

It was midnight. Time for him to get to bed. But he knew sleep wouldn't come tonight. Not after the events of today.

He'd not even called Troy or Shayne to let them know the news.

He was still smarting from the embarrassment of losing a case to her, especially one as minor as this one.

But he still couldn't get over seeing Rachel after thirteen years. He had tried to bury her in his memories but had failed. There were too many places in Barbados significant to them. It was difficult to avoid.

Anger boiled inside. He thought he hated her for what she'd done to him, but today he realized he didn't hate her, couldn't hate her.

His attraction to her was something he had not expected, but maybe it was just feelings based on nostalgia, on those tender memories from his past. In a few weeks, he'd be accustomed to seeing her. He just needed to remember that she had married another man.

The phone rang, interrupting his thoughts. He glanced at the display.

Shayne. His friends always seemed to call at the times he needed them most.

"You're all right?" So Shayne had heard already.

"I'm good. Is this about Rachel?" he asked.

"Yes," Shayne confirmed. "A lawyer friend called me today. Told me she saw your ex-girl in court."

"Already? That was fast. By now the whole island must know."

Shayne laughed.

"Did she tell you Rachel wupped my ass too?"

"She did? You actually lost a case?"

"Yes. Her first case since her return and she beats me."

"She must be good. You haven't lost a case in ages."

"She is good," George replied. "I underestimated my opponent...."

"That's good. Rivalry like old times. She should keep you on your toes."

"You're trying to say I'm not doing my job well?" he scoffed.

"No, definitely not."

"So what do you mean then?"

"You've changed. You've lost your passion for your work. Oh, you're still doing what you have to do, but you used to be on fire for each of your cases. I don't see that anymore."

George didn't reply at first. He didn't want to admit it, but what Shayne said was true. Every day he felt as if he were going through the motions. Maybe he needed a break.

"Maybe you need a break," Shayne echoed his thoughts.

"Maybe I do," he replied.

"Sorry to cut this conversation short, but my son is calling me."

"You go ahead, Papa. I have some work to do. But we have to get together sometime."

"Definitely. I'll call you in a few days."

He put the phone down, feeling a sense of loss. He needed to go and see his godchildren. He hadn't seen them for a couple of weeks. And with Troy's fiancée, Sandra, pregnant too, there were more godchildren on the way.

Years ago, he'd expected that by now he'd have kids. He'd spoiled it all when he had made it clear that his career came first. He had given up love for a dream—one that didn't even give him satisfaction anymore.

He imagined what it would be like to have a child. His son would probably be going off with Shayne and his son to play cricket. He'd make sure his son loved cricket, even though he wouldn't have to. Any son of his would have cricket in his genes.

He walked over to the door that led to the balcony. He knew that he needed to eat, but he wasn't in the mood. Maybe later.

He walked out onto the balcony. The sun was setting.

It was his favorite time of the day. He didn't make it home early too often, but when he did, he never failed to experience the beauty that came with a sunset.

For a while he was lost in the awesomeness of nature's handiwork, a kaleidoscope of vibrant color.

When it was finally dark and only a small handful of stars flashed in the sky, he finally acknowledged that he needed to deal with Rachel's return home.

How on Earth had his life suddenly become so complicated?

Chapter 4

Rachel woke the next day, her body groaning from lack of sleep. She'd tossed and turned into the early hours of the morning, and when she did fall asleep, it had been a fitful one, filled with dreams of George. As the sun forced its way between the delicate curtains in her room, she woke all hot and bothered. It was not only her attraction to him that worried her, but also the impending dilemma that would result when George discovered he had a twelve-year-old son.

She hoped that time would be later rather than sooner, but the island was too small and her secret could not remain that way; it was an inevitability.

She rose slowly from her bed. She woke Gregory and then checked on her mother, who was feeling much better but had agreed to rest during the day and make an appointment for the doctor.

Two hours later she entered her office, having

dropped Gregory off at school. The car service collected him on evenings and dropped him home. Her job as a prosecutor demanded long hours. She rarely left the office before the streetlights came on. She was fortunate to have most weekends and all holidays off. Those days, she devoted to her son.

Her day was pretty uneventful, but just before she was about to leave for home, her boss called her into his office. Her body shook with anticipation. Something good was about to happen.

She stepped into the cool, air-conditioned office and glanced at the handsome black man who sat there. When he looked up, he smiled at her. In his mid-fifties, Carlos Thorne looked way younger. He ran the department with an iron fist but was fair and easy to get along with.

"I know you've only been here for a few weeks now, but your reputation as a prosecutor in Anguilla was definitely a factor in our hiring you so easily. You're familiar with the Donovan case Bryan is working on?"

"Yes, I've heard about it. It's been all over the news," she replied.

"Well, this is going to be a very difficult one. Bryan is the lead on this case, but he needs to have surgery in a few days and will be out from work for the next five or six months. The trial is coming up and I want you to take over. Your life is going to be turned upside down. You're going to have to eat and drink this trial." His eyes focused on her, probing, as if waiting to see her reaction.

Rachel could not breathe. She couldn't believe that the trial of the year had dropped into her lap.

"I would be honored," she said without hesitation. "I appreciate your confidence in me, sir."

"Good. Then that's settled. I want you to do a good job. Don't let me regret giving it to you. I'm getting some political pressure, but I want that man convicted. Just because Donovan is a politician doesn't give him a free reign to murder and get away with it. He has one of the best criminal lawyers on the island. Maybe the fact that you beat him just yesterday will give you a psychological advantage."

The color drained from her face. A trial like this was a bit too good to come without complications. Now she'd have to deal with George in court.

"You should go talk to Bryan before you leave. Friday is his last day at work, so he will bring you up to speed with the case."

"Will do, sir," she replied, torn between dread at having to face George each day and excitement for the upcoming trial.

Rachel headed immediately to Bryan's office, unable to contain her excitement. She wanted to get started as soon as possible.

Later, as she drove home, she kept thinking of the magnitude of the task before her. She stopped at Chefette to pick up the two pizzas she'd ordered. Since she was late, she didn't feel in the mood to cook and the files were beckoning her.

At home, she helped Gregory with his homework, and after sitting with her mother and son eating pizza and watching an episode of *House of Payne,* she eventually took a shower and headed back to the study.

Gregory was sitting at his desk. He looked up when

she entered. A frown lined his forehead. Something had upset him.

"What's wrong?" she asked.

"I don't want to make you angry," he responded, his voice low, almost a whisper.

"Why would I be angry?" she responded.

He shrugged.

"Talk to me, Gregory. You know you can talk to me about anything."

"I have a letter from the cricket coach for you. This weekend the coach wants to take us to the beach for training. He told us that our dads can come along. I don't have a dad anymore."

Rachel felt an ache so painful that she wasn't sure what to say.

"It hurts a bit, but I'll be all right," he said, looking up at her, tears pooled in his eyes. "Some of the other boys don't have dads either, so I won't feel left out. It just feels sad that my real dad didn't want me."

When she opened her arms, he stood, stepping into them willingly.

She hadn't realized that he had perceived what she had told him as rejection by his biological father.

She thought quickly but wasn't sure how to deal with the situation. Instead she held him until he pulled away and told her he was ready to finish his homework.

After they were done, he went off to bed. She could tell he was still sad and she hoped the hug she'd given him would offer him some comfort.

What was she going to do? She would have to make a decision soon. For now, she wasn't sure she was ready to tell George that he had a son.

She headed to her home office and took the files

from her briefcase. Hopefully, focusing on the upcoming trial would give her a few hours of relief.

Life was becoming more and more complicated and for the first time since her return home, she wondered if she had made the right decision to do so.

George watched from his bar stool as Troy and Shayne strolled into the sports bar as if they didn't have a care in the world. Tonight he was not quite in the mood for the company, but these times with his best friends were important, especially since Shayne didn't make it too often. At least seeing them dismissed his desire to go home and work.

On reflection, this regular Friday get-together was the only time he got to relax and socialize. His life had become so bogged down with work, and maybe that was the reason he wasn't enjoying it as much. This was the first time in four months they were meeting.

He was sure things would get even worse. Troy's wedding to his fiancée, Sandra Walters, was in a week's time. After that, George would be the only single one in the group.

"I'm so glad the two of you finally got here. I haven't eaten all day and this hunger is killing me," he said good-naturedly.

"You're going to have to stop doing that, partner," Troy commented. "If you don't, ulcers are going to start making a mess of your stomach. I'm a neurosurgeon so you better not come to me complaining. I don't do stomachs."

"So you get here thirty minutes late and then blame me for not eating," George replied, making a fist and punching Troy lightly on the chest.

"I've already ordered the usual. A large portion of those sumptuous barbequed ribs."

"And lots of French fries, right?" Shayne asked.

The waitress interrupted before he could reply. She escorted them to their table. There, she filled glasses with water and took orders for their drinks. Flashing a warm smile, she left with a promise to be back with their drinks and meal soon.

"So what's going on, boys?" Troy asked.

"The usual," Shayne said. "You know that the end of the harvest is particularly busy and stressful and with the bumper crop I have this year, I can't wait until it's over."

"I'm sure that Carla will be glad when it's over too," George commented. He turned to Troy. "And you, Troy. How are plans for the wedding going? When do we have to do the fitting for our suits?"

"Sandra promised to let me know by tomorrow. I'll call you as soon as I know." Troy sighed. "Boy, I didn't know that planning a wedding was so much trouble."

"Planning a wedding?" Shayne said, laughing loudly. "Sandra, Carla and Tamara are doing all the work, from what I've heard."

"So that's what Sandra's been telling you," Troy retorted. "I'm sure she hasn't told you that she has deprived me of my conjugal rights until the honeymoon. A whole week before I can get some! The nerve of that woman!"

"One week? And you're frustrated. I'm sure your hands are tired by now," George guffawed. "You need to exercise restraint."

"You can afford to say that," Troy replied. "You aren't getting much and no lady in her right mind will marry you." He paused. "Didn't mean to say that," he said apologetically.

"But it's true. I'm the single one and enjoying it."

Shayne broke the silence. "Troy, did he tell you that Rachel is back on the island?"

"Rachel? You mean Rachel Davis?" Troy's expression was priceless.

"Rachel St. Clair," Shayne corrected. "She married the old fart."

"Shayne, you don't have to rub in it, you know," Troy said. "The boy's still in love with her."

"Me?" George snapped. "You must be crazy! I don't feel anything for her."

"Methinks the boy protests too much," said Shayne. "We know you, George. You fell in love with her the first time you set eyes on her."

"But things have changed," George responded, trying to keep any emotion from his voice. "She's the one who went off and got married. And I'd be happy if we change the conversation."

"I agree," said Shayne. "Let's talk about something else."

"What about that trial you have coming up?" Troy asked. "It's going to be big. Everyone is talking about it."

"Remember what I told you the other night?" Shayne asked, looking directly at George.

"I remember," George replied.

"And what's that?" Troy asked. "You better not be keeping anything from me."

"It's fine, Troy. Shayne was talking to me about my work ethic. He believes I've lost my passion for my work. To be honest, I've just been going through the

To Love You More

motions. Hopefully, this trial will help me to refocus. This is a big case and I intend to win. Bryan is a great lawyer, but he hasn't beaten me in a case in years. I have the advantage."

"Just don't get too lackadaisical," Troy suggested. "Remember, you had your first defeat just yesterday."

"Okay, don't rub it in." He shrugged. "It wasn't that important of a case."

"See what I mean?" Shayne commented. "In the past, you would have considered all of your cases important."

"That's true, George," Troy emphasized.

"Okay, okay, you win," George said, his hands rising in defeat. "But I took your advice, Shayne. I used last night to reflect. With all that has been happening, I know I need to be more focused."

"So how does she look?" Troy asked.

"Who?" George asked.

"Rachel. Who else?"

"She looks fine," George replied abruptly.

"Fine. That's it? I'm sure she looks more than fine. She was always a sexy number. Didn't know what she saw in you."

They laughed, all except George. He didn't find their sense of humor at all amusing.

"Since you're men, you won't be able to appreciate my muscular sexiness. I can assure you that most women find me sexy, charming and a passionate lover. I'm a totally intense lover."

"Okay, okay, a bit too much information," Troy complained.

"Come off it, Troy," George snorted. "Remember that foursome we had…"

"Foursome?" Shayne asked. "What are you to talking about? This is the first time I'm hearing about this."

"Shayne, remember, you got married long before I did. I'm sure Carla would have had a problem with your joining us."

The waitress interrupted again and the scent of the barbequed ribs ended the conversation.

Two hours later and totally contented with the meal, the camaraderie and conversation, they left.

When George entered his home half an hour later, the answering machine was blinking. He checked his messages and immediately returned the call from his partner, Douglas.

Douglas answered the phone, his voice drowsy with sleep.

"What's so important that it can't wait until tomorrow?" George asked.

"A fact I now regret. I was dreaming about this woman with breasts like…."

"Douglas, the news?" George interrupted.

"Okay, okay. Bryan won't be the prosecuting lawyer anymore. Seems he's going to be off for six months having surgery."

"Who's replacing him?" he asked. He'd been looking forward to battling with Bryan.

"Rachel St. Clair, the new prosecutor. She's Judge Edward St. Clair's widow. They were living in Anguilla, but he died a few years ago. She recently returned to Barbados."

George almost slammed the phone down. This was getting worse.

"Thanks for letting me know," he said.

"I'm sure you have nothing to worry about, though I heard she's good."

"I know she's good," he responded. "Have a good night."

He put the phone down before Douglas could continue. He didn't want to be talking about Rachel St. Clair. She had just come back into his life and already things were becoming complicated.

His day had again gone from bad to worse. He seemed destined to come in contact with his ex-girlfriend. Fate seemed to enjoy toying with him.

He glanced at the clock on the wall. It was almost midnight, but he didn't have time to sleep. He'd spend a few hours scrutinizing the case file. Rachel had already proved herself a formidable opponent. He could not sit on his laurels. This trial would not be a walkover for him.

He headed down the hallway to his den, folding himself into his favorite chair.

The next few weeks were going to test his ability as a lawyer, but he expected that his emotional control was also going to be put to the test.

And Troy and Sandra's upcoming wedding didn't help him in any way. What Troy had said was very true. He'd be the only one not married.

Why on Earth did *she* have to return to Barbados? His life had been just fine when she was not around.

Her return only served to emphasize how lonely he was. And he hated being alone.

Chapter 5

The weeks before the trial passed quickly for Rachel, and she forced her mind to focus on the impending case. Fortunately, there was so much work to do, she didn't have time to think about the man she'd loved those many years ago.

She'd caught a glimpse of him in a feature in one of the local newspapers. He'd looked handsome in a black tuxedo as part of the groom's party at Troy's wedding.

The photo of a smiling Troy and his beautiful new wife had given rise to memories of a better time, so she tried to immerse herself even further in her work on the trial.

She tried to force images of the kissing and the passionate, intense lovemaking from her mind but it threatened to consume her. Each morning she would wake feeling grumpy and unfulfilled.

Even though she and Edward had eventually become

lovers during the later years of their marriage, he had never stirred her as a lover. Lovemaking had been a gentle habit. Though she'd enjoyed their relationship, the passion had never been there. He'd been good to her and in some ways she'd grown to love him. Her life with him had been safe—nothing like the feelings she was currently experiencing.

The first day of the trial, jury selection, dawned with a brilliant, tropical sky. The sun shone brightly, and outside her window birds sung melodies in keeping with the mood of expectancy.

She was confident she would win the case. She knew that only a great lawyer could get this defendant off, and she had prepared thoroughly, so George was in for a hard fight.

When she reached the courtroom, George was not there. Another strategy of hers. She always made it a policy to arrive in court before her opponents. It always left them feeling slightly intimidated when they entered after she did.

When George arrived fifteen minutes later, he immediately glanced in her direction. He hadn't expected her there, but he quickly regained his composure. First round goes to…Rachel St. Clair, as she had predicted.

By the end of the day, she was still feeling on top of the world. The jury selection was complete and the trial would begin the next day. During the selection, she'd won some and lost some, but she had the feeling that the jury would be a fair one. She suspected that George was feeling equally good.

As she walked along the corridor heading to the other side of the building where the prosecutors' offices were, she heard the staccato of footsteps behind her.

She stopped and turned to face the intruder, not surprised to see George.

He appeared calm, just as he had in court. Yet she'd noticed a greater sense of presence in him. There was a spark of excitement in his eyes she had not seen at the last trial.

"Rachel," he said when he reached her.

"George," she replied. "What can I do for you?"

"Nothing really. I just wanted to say hi."

"And you think that's a good idea? We're in the middle of a trial and we're on opposing sides. Experience should tell you that's not a good idea."

"How's your mom doing?" he asked, ignoring her comments.

She hesitated. She didn't want to know where he was going with this, but her mother had always liked him.

"She's not doing too well. She has been having frequent headaches. I've finally convinced her that she needs to see a doctor."

"I'm sorry to hear that. I've visited her a couple times over the years. She was still working the last time I spoke to her, but I'm assuming she's retired now."

"Yes, she retired about a year ago when she turned sixty. We're hoping the headaches are not serious."

He nodded sympathetically. "I'll try to come see her when the trial is over."

"No," she shouted, startling him with her response. "While I appreciate your concern, I'd prefer our contact to be work-related."

"We used to be friends, Rachel, long before we were lovers," he stated. "We can be friends, can't we?"

"I'm not sure about that," she said gently, looking him full in the eyes. "There are too many things in our past. I prefer my life to be void of conflict. This is a bit too unnerving right now."

"As you wish," he replied, his eyes emotionless. "I'll stay out of your way as much as possible. You have a good evening. Tell your mom I send my love."

She watched as he walked away, sadness weighing heavily on her heart. He had tried to appear indifferent to her rejection, but she knew the signs of his anger. The George she'd known would have had no problem with showing his anger.

But she couldn't feel sorry for him. She had to protect her son from him as long as possible. He had made it quite clear back then that he didn't want marriage or a family. She didn't want him to hurt her son.

Later that night, she turned into the driveway, glad to be finally home; the stress of the day's events had left her fatigued.

Her day's work still hadn't ended. She had to check on her mother, spend time with her son and then prepare for tomorrow's court session.

At least she'd be able to purge George's image from her mind for a few hours.

By the end of the two weeks of the trial, Rachel was exhausted but she was sure she'd done her best. Her closing arguments had been perfect, but George had done a great job too. She felt the jury would be on her side, but verdicts could be so unpredictable.

It was early afternoon when she received the call that she was needed back in court.

Minutes later, Rachel held her breath as the verdict

was read. She could not contain her excitement when the politician was found guilty. Her gaze immediately went in George's direction. What she saw there surprised her. He threw a grudging look of admiration her way, nodded and smiled.

She nodded in acknowledgment.

When her co-council asked her to step outside for the press conference, she complied.

The steps of the courthouse were a hive of excitement. Police officers tried, with little success, to keep the crowd under control. When the reporters saw her, they rushed in her direction, shoving microphones rudely at her.

She stepped back, raising her hands, insisting on a semblance of order. The crowd settled slowly; the noisy buzz dimmed until there was silence.

Rachel made her brief statement and answered the questions posed to her. Thanking the media, she glanced to the left and saw George standing a short distance away.

He was alone.

A sense of longing gripped her and she walked toward him, startled when a young man rushed toward her, screaming loudly.

In his hand, the blade of a knife flashed menacingly.

Instinctively, Rachel shifted her body, but the outstretched hand plunged forward. Pain, red-hot pain, startled her with its strength. Her knees buckled and she started to fall, raising her hands in anticipation of another stab.

Instead, nothing came and she crumbled slowly to the ground, the darkness, ominous and overpowering, consuming her. Urgent hands grabbed for her and the last thing she remembered hearing was the fear in George's voice as he shouted, "Call an ambulance!"

The waiting room in the E.R. was surprisingly empty. George stood for the hundredth time and then sat again. He felt helpless. What could he do? He needed to call Rachel's mother, but he didn't have a number for her in his cell phone.

His body shook with the fear he'd experienced when the man had raced toward Rachel. George had acted on pure instinct. He didn't know he could move so quickly. Just as the man was about the plunge the knife for the second time, he had tackled him to the ground.

Other hands had helped subdue the man and George had moved quickly to Rachel's side where she lay on the steps, a bloodstain spreading across her white blouse.

When the ambulance had arrived, his hands, numb with pain, still pressed two handkerchiefs against the wound, stemming the flow of blood.

The short drive to the hospital had been nerve-wracking. He'd refused to leave her, taking control at the hospital and shouting orders like a tyrant, until the doctor in charge had asked security to intervene.

Now, sitting in the waiting room of the E.R., he pulled his cell phone from his pocket. He needed to call Shayne and Troy. He needed to change his shirt and get someone to collect his car. He needed to…

He closed his eyes, riding the wave of nausea that washed over him. He breathed deeply and slowly until his stomach settled.

His hands shaking, he punched in Troy's number. Troy answered on the first ring, an unusual occurrence. He sighed in relief.

"Troy, are you at the hospital?" he asked.

"Yes. What's wrong?"

"Rachel's been stabbed. I'm in the E.R. She's in surgery."

"I'll be there." The phone went silent.

Tension flowed from his body. It was good having a doctor as a best friend. Troy would know what to do.

Two minutes later, Troy walked through the "Staff Only" door, his cell phone to his ears. On seeing George, he ended the call.

"I just called Shayne. He'll be here as soon as he can. You stay here and I'll go and find out what's happening." Troy touched his hand briefly, and its warmth offered comfort. Troy was here. Things would be all right.

Troy turned and disappeared through the door.

George sat slowly. He glanced around the room. A few anxious faces, like his, glanced around the room, looking nowhere and everywhere.

The images of what had happened played across his mind's eye like the trailer from a movie. In all his life, he had never experienced a fear so intense. He had felt helpless and lost. Time had stopped and all he could think of was that he had to save Rachel. He had to stop the man intent on killing her.

Fifteen minutes later, Troy reappeared.

George jumped up. "How is she doing?" he asked.

"I haven't heard anything much yet. She is still in surgery."

He sat without responding. The waiting was killing him. Troy lowered himself into the next chair.

"She's going to be all right," Troy reassured him. "She's in good hands. Dr. Roland Thomas is the best. If there is anyone who can save her, it's him."

He was about to respond when the doors of the E.R. slid apart and Shayne stepped inside.

"How is she?" he asked.

"I'm not sure," George responded.

"She's still in surgery," Troy added.

Shayne sat. "What happened?"

George related the story, remaining as brief as he could. When he was done, he sat back, closing his eyes. Reliving the event was not easy.

"You've had something to eat?" Shayne's voice broke the silence.

He realized that he had not eaten since he had left home that morning. With his focus on the case and now Rachel, he'd clearly forgotten. A nagging hollowness in his stomach signaled his hunger.

"No, but I'm not sure I can eat anything right now."

"You need to eat," Shayne insisted. "I'll go to the canteen and get a sandwich for you." He turned to Troy. "You need something?"

Troy shook his head. "I ate just before I came downstairs."

"Good. Troy, you take care of him for me. I'll be back."

When Shayne left, George sat quietly, his thoughts on Rachel. He couldn't lose her a second time. He'd realized something in that moment when the attacker had raised the knife. He would have died for Rachel. She'd been his lover, but she'd also been his friend and no matter what had happened between them, they needed to let bygones be bygones.

He turned to Troy. "Thanks for coming."

"Come off it, George." Troy scoffed. "What else did you expect me to do? We've been best friends forever, remember? Haven't we always been here for each other?"

"I know. I'm just glad you and Shayne are here."

"You still care about her?" Troy asked.

"It's that obvious?" he replied.

"Yeah."

"I know I can't lose her again. I'm not sure if this is a second chance I have, but when she's all right, I'm going to do everything in my power to win her back."

Another sound of footsteps. He looked up. A doctor was walking toward them.

Troy stood immediately. George followed suit.

"Roland, is she all right?" Troy asked.

"She's going to be fine, Troy," the doctor responded. "Though the wound was deep, there was no damage to any vital organs. She did lose a lot of blood, but the paramedics say that the man who came to her rescue did a good job of controlling the bleeding. He saved her." He glanced at George's shirt. "That must be you."

George nodded.

"I expect her to be here for a few days," the doctor continued. "She can go home then, but she has to take things easy."

"Can I see her?" George asked anxiously.

"Yes, of course," he responded. "She's still out from the effect of the anesthetic. She'll probably sleep for the rest of the night."

"I'd like to see her now."

"That's fine. Troy can take you up to her room. She gave your name and her mother's before her surgery. She said I should ask you to contact Mrs. Davis." He pulled a sheet of paper from his board and handed it to George.

George turned to Troy. "Can we go now?" He didn't want to wait. He wanted to see her as soon as possible.

"Let's go," Troy said, leading the way.

When he stepped inside the room, he shivered. On the bed, Rachel lay still, too still, but when he moved closer, the rise and fall of her chest reassured him she was alive.

Damn, he was being paranoid. He sighed deeply. Her caramel complexion seemed even paler, but her breathing was soft and steady.

Unexpected tears stung his eyes. He seemed unable to control their flow.

The realization that he'd almost lost her tormented him. He'd never stopped loving her.

He whispered a soft prayer upward. He'd been given a second chance and he had almost lost her again.

A sharp pain tightened his chest and he could not breathe. He turned and rushed out of the room. He had to get away.

Outside, he breathed in deeply, trying to bring his body under control. He glanced along the corridor. It was quiet. No one had seen his moment of weakness. But he realized something. He didn't care. He felt no shame in his display of emotion.

He remembered he had not called Rachel's mother. He pulled out the paper Dr. Thomas had given him and dialed the number.

Her mother picked up on the first ring.

"Mrs. Davis, this is George."

"George?" she said cautiously.

"George Simpson."

"George, I haven't heard from you in ages. How are you doing? Rachel's not here."

"I know she isn't there, Mrs. Davis. I have some news for you. Rachel had an incident this afternoon. I couldn't call you before because I didn't have your contact information. She's at the hospital and has had surgery, but she's all right now, so there is no need for you to worry."

"Oh, dear. I'll get my neighbor to bring me to the hospital. Which ward is she in?"

"Ward B5. I'll wait until you get here."

"Thanks for calling. I'll be there as soon as I can."

"I'll be here." He disconnected the call.

He walked briskly back down the corridor to the waiting room.

He found Shayne and Troy chatting. Upon seeing him, they beckoned him to an empty chair next to where they were sitting.

He sat, the aroma of food causing his stomach to grumble.

"She looks fine. She is still unconscious, but she's breathing easily. Her mother is on her way here, so I'll use that time to go home, take a shower and come back. I'll take a few days off from work so I can be here."

"Good, but you need to eat this," Shayne said, handing him a brown bag.

He opened it and took the sandwich out. He devoured it quickly.

As he'd expected, his friends made no comment about his situation. He didn't have to tell them anything and even if they found his involvement surprising, they would leave him to do what he had to.

When he was done eating, he turned to them, and smiled weakly. "Thanks again for being here."

"You know it's no problem, George," Troy responded, a hand reaching out to pat him on the back.

They sat quietly, occasionally one of them making a random comment.

When Rachel's mother appeared, he walked quickly to greet her.

Mrs. Davis immediately started to cry.

He placed his hands around her, holding her closely and offering what comfort he could. When she'd stopped crying, he, with Shayne and Troy, took her up to the room where Rachel still lay asleep.

Mrs. Davis had added some personal touches to the room. Flowers of all colors bloomed in a small vase. A gift basket of local fruit had been placed on the tiny dresser.

George glanced across at Rachel where she lay asleep. She'd been sleeping for almost twelve hours now and he wondered when she would wake. He needed to see her open her eyes before he could totally relax.

He rose slowly from the chair. Fortunately, it was comfortable, but his body was sore from the long hours sitting. He had drifted off to sleep for a while, but for the past thirty minutes he'd been wide awake.

He sorted through the fruit, finally settling on a golden apple and a few grapes. He hoped Mrs. Davis wouldn't mind, but he was hungry.

He was returning to the chair when a soft whimper came from the bed. He turned toward the sound. She was awake. His heart soared.

Rachel slowly opened her eyes and glanced around

the room, her gaze landing on him. Her face contorted in confusion.

"Where am I?" she asked, her voice raspy. She shifted and grimaced in pain.

He moved quickly to her side, his hand resting on her shoulder. He couldn't bear to see her in pain, but he was helpless about what to do.

"You're in the hospital," he replied gently.

Realization changed her expression to one of distress.

"The man...he stabbed me," she accused.

"Yes, but you had surgery and are okay."

"It hurts," she said.

"Do you need me to call the nurse?" he asked.

"No," she said, her voice labored and strained. "I'll be all right."

"Well, just let me know if you need someone."

She whispered something in reply, and he moved closer. He could tell she was already tired.

"Water," she rasped.

He glanced around, noticing a pitcher and glass.

He reached for the glass and filled it. He raised her to a sitting position and handed her the glass. She took it and raised it to her head, drinking deeply until all was gone. She handed the empty glass to him.

"More?" he asked.

She shook her head, resting back against the pillow. "Thanks," she said. Her eyes closed slowly, the hint of a smile on her face.

He watched her until she fell asleep. He glanced at his watch. One o'clock.

He needed to go home and get some rest and return in the morning. He would drop by the office to make sure all was well and then he would come back.

He glanced at her one last time before he left. When he reached the door, he turned around and walked back to the bed. He bent and kissed her gently on her cheek.

He loved her.

During the night, Rachel came suddenly awake. Her body shivered with a fear of the unknown. Where was she?

As she glanced around, images flashed in her mind's eye…standing on the steps of the courthouse, the bright flash of the knife, the pain, George standing with her.

She tried to raise herself up, but excruciating pain pierced her side.

She almost cried out but stifled the sound.

Where was George? What was he doing? Had her mother been told? She hoped so. She remembered that George had been there when she'd first opened her eyes in the fogging nothingness. She was sure he would have made contact with her mother.

She glanced around the room. She was thirsty. She tried to shift herself off the bed, but the pain was too unbearable. She searched for the ringer, found it and pressed it to summon the nurse.

A few minutes later, the nurse entered her room.

"So you're finally up, Ms. Davis. I'm sure you want something to eat and to take care of nature's calling."

Rachel could only nod.

Twenty-five minutes later, feeling refreshed and less burdened by nature, she rested her head against the pillow.

She'd been informed by the nurse that her mother had been there for several hours and would return in the morning and that she was not to worry, that Gregory was fine.

She sighed in relief. Her mother and son were her major concern. She didn't worry about work; she knew things would be taken care of. She wondered about the extent of the damage, but since she was alive, she suspected that the damage had been minimal.

With each moment she remembered more of the incident and knew that George had saved her life. She remembered clearly that he had pounced on her attacker before she had succumbed to darkness.

George.

The name rang in her ears.

Things were getting a lot more complicated than she'd expected.

How could she continue with her plan to ignore him and keep their relationship professional? The man had saved her life. That, at least, indicated that she had to extend a hand of friendship, even if she needed to be cautious.

But she would still try to keep him at arm's length for a while. She didn't want him at her home. She shifted on the bed, which gave rise to a sharp stab of pain.

She inhaled deeply, riding out the pain. Already her body was feeling tired again.

Sleep descended slowly and she closed her eyes, the image on her mind one of a brave man who had saved her life.

Chapter 6

When Rachel woke the next time, her mother was sitting in her room, her eyes closed, her lips moving. She was praying.

Soft rays of sunlight eased their way between the dark curtains. She shifted her body, sore from lying on the bed for so long. Pain coursed up her side. She breathed deeply, waiting for it to subside.

Despite the pain, she closed her eyes, sending her own words of prayer upward. She was glad to be alive.

Outside she could hear the low hum of vehicles driving by the Queen Elizabeth Hospital, the sole government-owned hospital on the island, nestled on the outskirts of the city of Bridgetown.

Her mother opened her eyes, rising from the chair when she realized her daughter was awake.

"Oh, sweetheart, are you all right? Do you need a nurse?"

"I'm fine, Mother. I'm feeling better."

"I can't believe what happened. Things like this don't happen in Barbados," she sobbed.

"Mom, there is no need to cry," Rachel reassured. "I haven't spoken to the doctor yet, but the nurse told me I'll be fine. The knife did not damage any vital organs."

"I know it. God listens. He knows you have a young son to take care of."

She nodded, acknowledging her mother's words. Maybe God did listen. Rachel knew she had come close to being an annual statistic.

"The nurse told me to call her when you wake up. She came with your breakfast but you were still sleeping."

"Yes, I'm a bit hungry, but before you go, I need to find out how Gregory is doing."

"He's worried, but I told him you'll be all right. He's next door at Marjorie's. He doesn't seem to mind spending the time there since he and Jonathan are friends."

"Thanks, Mom, for taking care of everything."

"It's not me. You have your young man to thank. He was here last night," she replied. And almost as an afterthought, she said, "A boy needs to know his father."

"Please don't go there, Mom."

"Just my opinion, sweetheart."

She paused. Her mother didn't deserve her attitude.

"Sorry I snapped at you, Mom," she said, "but I'd prefer not to deal with that for now."

Her mother glanced at her watch. "I'm going to have to go. Marjorie's husband is coming for me soon. I'll be back this evening. I spoke to your doctor and he says you need to be here a few days. You'll be in pain for a bit, but you'll heal."

Her mother bent and kissed her on the cheek.

"Give Gregory my love. I'll call him at Marjorie's," she told her mother.

"Yes, he keeps asking if you're all right. Bye, honey. I'll let the nurse know you're ready for breakfast," she said as she walked out of the room.

Rachel shifted slowly and reached for the phone.

Their neighbor picked up immediately.

"Marjorie, this is Rachel. Thanks for taking care of Gregory for me."

"It's no problem. He's a good boy and Jonathan has been delighted to have him over. He's here having breakfast. How are you doing?"

"I'm not too bad. At least nothing serious was damaged."

"That's good. We were worried about you. Hold on, I'll let Gregory talk to you. He's staring at me. I suspect he knows it's you."

"Hi, Mom." Her son's voice came over the line.

"Hi, sweetheart."

"Mom, you're all right?" he asked. "They talked about you on the news last night. You're not going to die, are you?"

"No, Gregory," she reassured him. "I'm going to be fine."

"Scout's honor?" he asked, using his favorite phrase.

"Yes, Scout's honor," she replied.

"When are you coming home? I miss you."

"It'll be soon. But in the meantime, don't give your grandmother any trouble."

"You know I won't, Mom."

She smiled. It was true. Her son was a bit too perfect. But in today's world, that wasn't a bad thing.

"Good, you go finish your breakfast. Your grand-mother is on the way home, but since it's Saturday, you can stay there with Jonathan. Let me talk to Marjorie again."

"Bye, Mom. Love you."

"Love you too," she replied before Marjorie came back on the line.

"I hope it's okay if Gregory stays there today?" she asked.

"Oh, I've already told his grandmother he can stay here as long as he wants. In fact, he says he doesn't mind, but he has to be at home to sleep with his grand-mother at nights."

Rachel experienced a surge of pride.

She laughed. "Thanks, Marjorie. I know it can't be easy to have two energetic boys around."

"They are no trouble, dear. Gregory is welcome here anytime."

"Thanks again. The nurse just walked in with my breakfast. I'll see you when I get back home."

She hung up and turned to the smiling nurse.

Half an hour later, her body refreshed from a shower and breakfast, she rested her head on the pillow. She'd asked the nurse for one of the local papers, but she was already feeling a bit tired.

She wondered when George was going to come again, or if he already felt he'd done the neighborly thing and that was enough?

A part of her wanted to see him again, but she was being silly. Maybe the accident had affected her. She was feeling helpless and vulnerable. Maybe his not being around was a good thing.

She had no intention of falling in love with him again. It would be madness.

George walked along the empty corridor, the sound of his footsteps echoing loudly. Trepidation slowed his steps. While he wanted to see Rachel, he was reluctant to face her. Not that he was afraid of her or anything. It was his feelings for her. He couldn't stop thinking about her, of what he'd missed.

Yes, he was concerned for her, but there were questions that remained unanswered. Answers he needed to know if he wanted to leave that part of his life behind.

He didn't expect a return to that relationship. Her feelings for him may be nothing like they had been, but he could not ignore the flash of desire he'd seen in her eyes. It had been a fleeting moment of vulnerability, he suspected, but he'd seen it nevertheless.

Outside her room, he paused, uncertain of her reaction to his arrival. He *had* saved her life. She could not ignore that. He would even use it to dismiss any objections to his visit.

He knocked on the door and pushed it open slowly.

Damn, she was beautiful. For minutes they stared at each other, both unsure of what to say. His heart was pounding in his chest. He smiled, hoping that it would give him confidence, but inside his heart fluttered with excitement.

Rachel smiled in return, a lopsided, cautious smile that didn't quite reach her eyes. For a moment he saw a glimpse of fear and wondered what could cause her to be afraid of him, but as quickly as he saw it, it was gone, and he wondered if he'd been imagining things.

"How are you feeling this morning?" he asked politely.

"I'm doing fine. I slept well last night after the nurse give me a painkiller. It hasn't been too bad since I woke up."

"That's good to hear. Did you see your mother?"

"Yes, she was here when I woke this morning. She told me you were here earlier…that you called her."

"I was glad to help," he replied. "Someone needed to let her know."

"Thank you. I really appreciate it." She paused, as if trying to find the right words. "I want to thank you for saving me yesterday. I could have died."

"It was nothing. I was glad I was out there at the time. Your attacker was acting suspicious. I'm sorry I didn't respond quicker."

"There is no need to worry about what else you could have done. Have the police found out who he is? Why he attacked me?" she asked.

"They haven't told you yet?" he replied. "His name is Brown. You handled his wife's divorce a few weeks ago. She had left the island with the kids the day he attacked you. He blames you for their leaving. He was definitely trying to kill you."

She remained silent. He could tell she was internalizing all he had said.

"So I owe you my life," she said eventually.

"Rachel, you owe me nothing. I would have done the same thing for anyone." He stopped, realizing what he'd said when he saw the hurt in her face.

"I didn't mean it that way. Whatever has happened between us, you were my friend. Based on what you've said, there may be no way to repair what happened between the two of us, but can't we just be friends again? I'm willing to leave the past behind. We have to be bigger than that."

She hesitated for the briefest of moments, then nodded slowly. "I'll think about it. Although what you say is true, I don't want to be reminded every day what I did to you or what you did to me. That type of thinking only leaves you constantly knocking yourself. I have no intention of doing that."

"That's all I can expect from you." He glanced down at his watch. "I just dropped by to see how you were doing. I have to head into the office for a bit. I've taken a few days off. I'll come by later."

She hesitated before she responded. "Okay, and thanks for coming."

"Shayne and Troy say they'll visit sometime today."

"I'd love to see them. I haven't seen them in ages."

"I'll see you later." He stepped forward and, on instinct, lowered his head and placed a soft kiss on her lips.

Heat flared between them and the kiss intensified, until he pulled away, flustered and excited by what had happened.

"You have a good day," he finally said, sounding a lot more confident than he was feeling.

He turned and walked out of the room, aware of her eyes on him. What on Earth had he done? He hoped he wouldn't live to regret his impulsiveness.

But as he walked along the corridor, he was aware of something most powerful.

The passion between them was still there and the temptation to revive what they'd had was powerful.

That much he was sure of.

* * *

Rachel sighed when the door closed behind him. The craving flowing through her body had startled her with its intensity. She'd had to control her response to him, but she had to admit that the attraction she felt for him, had always felt for him, still remained.

She raised her hands to her lips. His touch still lingered. Inside she yearned for more. The unexpected kiss had left her languishing.

What was she going to do?

She closed her eyes, resting her head against the pillow.

She'd go back to sleep. Sleep was the best cure for recovery and buried memories that threatened one's equilibrium.

There was a knock on the door and a nurse she'd not seen before walked in.

"I just came in to let you know there are two friends outside to see you."

"Who are they?" she asked.

"One is Dr. Whitehall. I'm not sure who the other person is."

"You can let them come in."

"Your doctor will be here in an hour or so." She turned and walked out.

After a knock on the door, Shayne and Troy walked in.

Rachel wasn't sure what to say, but the smiles on their faces were enough to let her know that everything was all right between them.

"So how is our girl doing?" Troy asked, bending to kiss her on the cheek. Shayne followed suit.

Before she could respond, the most embarrassing thing happened. She started to cry.

Standing on opposite sides of the bed, they each held one of her hands.

Shayne's expression was one of concern, while Troy treated her like one of his patients, his voice calm and soothing.

After the tears finally abated, Rachel raised her head, embarrassed at what had happened.

"You're going to be all right," Troy said. "I spoke to Dr. Thomas, who happens to be a good friend of mine. He says you'll be here for a few days and then you'll be back at home."

"That's good to hear," she said with a quick laugh.

"Heard you've been wupping George in the court-room," Shayne said, patting her on the shoulder.

"Just beginner's luck," she replied modestly.

"Beginner's luck?" Shayne responded. "I heard you're dynamic in court. Maybe our dear friend will sit up and take notice. He didn't know what hit him."

"George is good in court too," she emphasized. "It was exhilarating watching him. I still can't believe I won."

"Well, he did spend a few days sulking after that first trial. This time, your misfortune has kept his mind off of being trounced again."

"I'm glad my demise was of some benefit," she said good-naturedly.

For a moment there was silence.

"So how have you been?" Troy asked, pausing immediately. "Stupid question, right? You just got hurt. I meant since we last saw you almost thirteen years ago."

"It *has* been a long time," Shayne emphasized. "I missed you."

"Yeah, I missed you too," Troy repeated.

Her face turned red. She hadn't expected such sentiments. A lump of guilt stuck in her throat, delaying her reply.

"I'm sure my going to Anguilla is no secret. A pretty uneventful few years. I started practicing about four years ago after Edward passed away. The first years there I stayed at home..." She coughed, covering the statement she had almost made.

"Are you all right?" Troy asked, holding her gently until the bout of coughing subsided. "We really shouldn't keep you any longer. You can tell us all about your life in Anguilla another time."

"I am feeling a bit tired," she replied.

"I'm at work for the rest of the day, so I'll drop by soon and we'll talk. We have a lot of catching up to do," Shayne said.

"Definitely. It was really nice of you to come visit me."

"You're our friend, Rachel. We don't know exactly what happened between you and George, but that is something the two of you will have to work out. The only thing you didn't do was trust us enough to tell us what was going on."

"I'm sorry," she said sadly. "One day I'll have to tell you both."

"That's good enough for me," Shayne replied.

"Me too," Troy said, reaching to hold her hands in his. "I would be lying if I said we didn't want to know."

"Speak for yourself, Troy. As I said, that's between Rachel and George."

"And you have to promise me something. When you're better, I'm going to invite everyone over for dinner. You have to get to know the wives and kids."

"Kids? I knew Shayne was married and I saw Troy's photos in the paper, but I didn't realize both of you had kids."

"Well, I have the wife and kids, and Troy's wife is expecting. You remember my sister, Tamara, and brother, Russell. They are both married too. Tamara is a vet and lives on the island with her husband, Kyle. Russell is married to Tori Matthews and lives in the U.S."

"You mean Tori Matthews the singer?" she asked, unable to contain her excitement.

"Yes, that's the one."

"I can't believe it. I love her music." In her excitement, she moved awkwardly and winced in pain.

"I guess this is the perfect time to say goodbye. I have to get back to work and I'm sure Troy does too. You need to get some rest."

Troy glanced at his watch. "That's true. It's soon time for my rounds. I have a few patients to check on."

"It's great that you followed your dream," Rachel observed. "That is what you always wanted."

"Most of us did get to do what we wanted. Thought Shayne wanted to be an engineer, but at least he's happy running the most successful sugar plantation on the island."

"Yeah, I'm happy, but no more talking, Rachel. We're going to leave you and let you have some rest." He bent to kiss her on her forehead. Troy did the same.

"Of course, since I work here, I'll try to check in on you later, but you'll be here for a few more days."

She nodded. "Thanks for dropping by. I'm feeling a lot better now, but I think I need to get a little rest. I get tired easily."

"Yes, you get some rest. Remember you lost a lot of blood."

Shayne waved and followed Troy out the door.

Rachel closed her eyes and rested her head against the pillow. She'd overdone it. She *was* feeling really tired.

Her feelings warred with each other. She had been happy to see Shayne and Troy and hadn't expected them to be so warm and friendly. Their coming back into her life only further complicated her current situation with George. The sense of impending doom was overwhelming. Gregory's discovery was inevitable.

For now she would play things by ear. She only hoped George didn't hate her when he found out.

When George reached the hospital later that day and walked into Rachel's room, he was surprised to see her sitting in the chair watching television.

She turned in his direction when he entered, her eyes guarded, as if she wanted to keep him out. Disappointment washed over him, his excitement at seeing her dissipating. He suspected she'd thought long and hard about his proposal.

"I can leave if you'd prefer me not to be here," he blurted out. He was not one to pretend that his visit was the highlight of her day.

She appeared shocked at his suggestion. "I'm sorry, I didn't mean to be rude. I didn't realize that my response to your entry was so noticeable."

"I can read people easily. It's a skill we both have,

don't we?" he said calmly. He didn't want this anger between them. "And since we're not beating about the bush, toying with each other, you can tell me what you decided."

She paused briefly.

"Although I appreciate that we were friends years ago and we're back in each other's lives, I'm not sure there is a need for us to become all chummy again. I would really prefer if we remain just colleagues. Too much hurt is there in the past and I'm not in the mood for us getting all psychological and sharing our motivations for what we did back then."

He tried to speak and she lifted a finger.

"Let me finish what I have to say," she emphasized. "I know it has been all great to say 'let's be friends,' but both of us have moved on. You have your friends and I have mine. You've made a life of your own and so have I. We can't erase thirteen years of hurt so easily."

When he realized she was done, he said, "Then there is nothing for me to say. I respect your wishes. Since I know you're going to be okay, my work here is done. Of course, because we work in the same area, it's inevitable that we'll meet, but I will keep our contact to a minimum." He turned to leave. "Have a good day, Rachel."

And with that he was gone.

She was expecting relief, but Rachel felt as if she were reliving the past. The day she'd overheard him talking about his career and the obstacle she'd become flashed vividly in her mind.

George was definitely not father material. She would keep her son away from him as long as she could. She did not want him to hurt Gregory. She sighed. Keeping her relationship with George "strictly professional" was definitely for the best.

Her pain and sorrow was so profound it caused her body to shake and she began to cry.

She cried for the pain she'd just caused George. He'd reached out to her for forgiveness and she'd rejected him. She was scared. She'd seen and heard of too many situations like this one. Movies were fanciful, but she'd seen too many cases of men, like George, fighting for custody or partial custody of their offspring, and she had no doubt that George would fight her. Gregory would be sixteen in four years. He could make his own choices then.

Maybe she'd made a mistake. She should have remained in Anguilla, but her mother's plea for her to return had been too heart-wrenching. Her mother wanted her here, wanted them here. She wanted to see and spend time with her grandson and Rachel could not have denied her that wish.

She turned the television back on and tried to focus on the wacky comedy that was on.

But the only image she saw was that of George walking away and the pain she'd seen in his eyes.

That only made her own pain even worse.

What had she done?

George slammed the beer on the table. He didn't drink often but somehow he needed to wash away the day's disappointment. He was angry, more than angry.

He'd expected understanding from Rachel. The Rachel he'd known years ago had been more forgiving. This Rachel was different. She was colder, harder.

On the drive home, he'd thought about every word she'd said and with each minute his anger had grown.

In the quiet and comfort of his home, he knew he needed to calm himself. There was something more going on. He'd seen that flash of fear in her eyes. He would not rest until he discovered what was going on.

He'd give her time, but he had no intention of giving up. He had been given a second chance and until he knew for certain that things could not work between them he would fight for her.

His feelings for her had not changed. Even when he'd been in his early twenties and had broken their engagement, he'd known he loved her. He'd just wanted to give them time to grow up and embrace their dreams. He'd been too young, too unsure of what he really wanted in life.

The only person he had to blame was himself, but he had plans of rectifying that situation.

He closed the windows downstairs and made sure the security system was on. A bath, a few chapters of the book he was reading and then sleep.

Sleep?

Who was he trying to fool? He was probably being a bit optimistic. If he slept at all, he suspected his nights would be filled with dreams of Rachel just as they had been since he saw her that first day in the courthouse.

Tomorrow was another day.

Chapter 7

Rachel rose slowly from the sofa where she'd spent the past few hours fast asleep. She was bored. Her mother was cooking and Gregory was at school. Fortunately, it was two o'clock and he'd soon be home.

She walked over to the window, glancing outside and wondered if she should go and sit on the patio. She decided against it. There was no sense in going into the kitchen. Her mother wouldn't let her help. "You need to rest, honey," she kept saying.

But the inactivity was driving her crazy. She wasn't accustomed to sitting around doing nothing. Even when she'd first married Edward and was not working, she'd been occupied with taking care of Gregory. As soon as he'd entered kindergarten, she'd gone to work.

After spending five days in the hospital, she had been discharged. Today, Friday, a week after she'd been attacked, she was ready to go back to work.

Knowing that Carl Brown was behind bars gave her comfort. All indications suggested her attacker would plead guilty and she wouldn't have to deal with him.

Resting at home allowed her too much time to think about George and the past; every hour, every minute, every second of the day, his image bombarded, vivid, bold...and oh so appealing.

Her memories of him were not all bad. In fact, her memories of him were filled with mind-blowing lovemaking. George had been the perfect lover and, though it had taken her a long time to trust him, when she had given herself to him, she'd surrendered body and soul.

The soft, probing kiss he'd given her in the hospital had stoked flames she'd thought were long buried.

The first time they had made love she'd been excited and scared, but George had been gentle with her, encouraging her every step of the way, until she ached for him each day and he'd obliged willingly.

Now, the memories of their lovemaking created a longing deep inside her. Her last contact with a male body had been more than four years ago, before Edward had taken ill. Since then she had pushed her desire to the background, focusing on raising her son. Passion always resulted in pain and hurt, emotions she preferred to avoid.

Now, things were different. George had changed that.

She moved from the window, determined to ignore the memories. The sound of a key turning drew her from the memories. Gregory was home.

For a few hours, she would devote her time to him.

Along with her mother, Gregory was the only other person who mattered. No one else did.

And as the thought registered, she knew that she was lying to herself.

George dropped the bat on the bench and slipped out of his cricket whites. He walked naked across the changing room to the line of showers, his towel draped around his neck, not caring that the dressing room was filled with the members of his team.

People would probably think he was an exhibitionist, but he didn't really care. He'd always wondered why some men had a hang-up about nakedness or the size of their God-given tool. Weren't they all men?

He took the towel from around his neck and placed it on one of the available hooks. Cold water cooled his hot and exhausted body. He had enjoyed the Saturday-afternoon game and making his first fifty runs for the season was an added bonus. He had felt good batting on this particular pitch.

Today, for the first time in a long time, he'd felt the rhythm of the game. For him, the game of cricket was poetry in motion. His favorite cricketer, Brian Lara, exemplified this. When his hero held a bat in his hand, the combination of power and gracefulness made watching the talented player an awesome experience.

The game had helped to lift his dreadful mood. For the past week, he'd been unusually snappy and brash. Of course, everyone had noticed, and on Monday, when he returned to work, he owed several of his colleagues an apology.

What had come over him?

He suspected Troy and Shayne would have lots of

questions. They could tell he was unhappy about something and he would have to give them answers. They rarely hid anything from each other. With Kyle joining them this evening, he suspected that he'd have to brace himself for brotherly ribbing.

Sighing, he turned off the faucet. He dried his skin before he headed back to the changing room. Troy was already dressed and ready.

He dressed quickly, all the while listening to the idle banter between his teammates. He had never played cricket professionally, but he enjoyed playing with this team of cricket enthusiasts in a local, amateur competition. About five months ago he had finally convinced Troy to join them when he was off on Saturdays.

Fifteen minutes later, they were on the way to Bert's, their favorite sports bar and restaurant. George could already taste the sinfully delicious barbeque ribs he'd become addicted to. Since he had not eaten much during the day, the emptiness in his stomach had only become more aggravating while he'd been playing cricket.

"So you're okay, bro?" Troy asked. He could hear the concern in Troy's voice.

"Although I'd like to answer that question now, I'd rather respond when we get to Bert's. Shayne is bringing Kyle, so I know I'm going to have to explain to both of them too. So...why don't we just wait for me to get all weepy?"

"You, weepy?" Troy snorted. "That'll be a first." He paused. "You did cry in my arms many years ago," he said, humor in his voice.

"Don't remind me. I was a boy then. I won't be crying this time."

"Never say never, my boy. Real men don't have

a problem with crying. I've cried a few times. Can't promise I won't again. You never know what or who is going to re-enter your life."

"Touché, but I definitely don't have anything to cry about," he replied, his tone laced with disgust. "Right now, all I can think about is how hungry I am. I plan to eat all the ribs I can and drink myself into oblivion since you're driving."

"Um…George? You don't drink."

"The way I'm feeling, maybe I'll start tonight."

"Georgie Porgie's in love," Troy teased with a boyish grin.

"You laugh now, Dr. Whitehall. A few years ago you were the one dealing with your feelings. Now you and the wifey are expecting your first child. That's not going to happen to me. Remember, I love playing the field."

"You keep saying that, bro. It's just a matter of time." His laughter filled the car's interior.

"I hear you, but it's really time we change the conversation. How was your day at work?"

Troy laughed again. "Can't handle things when the pressure's on? How are you going to deal with Shayne and Kyle? You know they're going to ask."

"I'll deal with them when the time comes. I'm a lawyer, remember?"

"I remember. Let's hope your courtroom techniques work when we're interrogating."

George did not respond. He turned his gaze out the windows. The highway stretched before them, cars snaking their way home. Exiting the highway at the Sagicor roundabout, the car traveled down Rendezvous

Hill and then along the south coast until Troy finally pulled into the bar's parking lot.

As if on cue, George's stomach rumbled.

Damn, he was hungry.

"Shayne's car is already here," Troy observed. "I hope we haven't kept them waiting too long."

"I doubt that. Not that it matters anyway. Shayne's a stickler for time. Sometimes he needs to loosen up."

"True," Troy responded, pulling the car into a spot next to Shayne's Toyota Camry.

With the car parked and locked, they walked into the lively establishment. George loved the warm, noisy atmosphere. Even the sound of multiple sports channels offered comfort with its familiarity.

Immediately, they picked up Shayne and Kyle sitting at their regular, poolside table.

Reaching their friends, George sat. There was a rumbling from the area of George's stomach.

Shayne laughed. "I see you're still not eating when you should. You workaholics need to take time to eat. It can't take a whole hour to eat."

"Look who's talking. You were no better. Now that you're domesticated and have a good wife, you're now an expert on eating habits," George replied, amusement in his voice. He turned to Kyle, who'd remained quiet during the exchange.

"So Kyle, how are the wifey and little ones doing?"

Kyle smiled, his face lighting up at the mention of his loved ones. "Great. Mya took her first step yesterday, so of course, Tamara told me I have to bring the photos for all of you to see."

He fumbled in his pocket and pulled an envelope out with an ease and flair that belied his blindness.

George grabbed for them first, receiving a thump in his side from Shayne, the proud uncle of the two little girls.

At times, as he looked at Kyle, he couldn't help but wonder how Kyle dealt with his blindness with such ease. In his late thirties, Kyle was still very handsome. George remembered the playboy, "playa" and spoiled cricketer who'd taken life so cavalierly. And then came the accident that had taken his sight and forced him to live like a recluse, until he'd met Tamara and she'd challenged him to be the man he'd finally become.

"George, stop daydreaming and take the photos," Troy said, giving him a thump on the other side.

"The two of you trying to kill me?" he replied good-naturedly, taking the photos from Shayne's outstretched hand.

"He's probably thinking about Rachel," Troy said.

George's breathing stopped. Here it comes. They couldn't even wait until after they ate.

He ignored the jab, scanning the photos and unable to hide his amusement and delight at Mya's first wobbly steps, her smile enchanting with her four teeth.

An emptiness he hadn't experienced before caused a tightness in his throat and he couldn't speak the words he wanted to.

"So what is this about a lawyer friend of George's?" Kyle asked again.

"Remember we chatted about George's ex-fiancée, Rachel, at Troy's wedding?" Shayne responded. "She was the prosecutor who was stabbed recently outside the courthouse."

"I didn't realize that was her. Wasn't she Rachel Davis?" Kyle asked. "And I'm now hearing this?"

"She was Davis, but she got married. And I did tell Tamara to let you know about the incident," he said.

"You know Tamara's brain. She remembers the names of all the animals in the clinic, but if she has to remember a simple message, she's lost."

They laughed.

"So there is hope that we'll see another one of us married sometime soon," Shayne said.

"I don't know about that," Troy said. "He claims that he's not in love with her anymore."

"Sure," Kyle interjected. "He's had the hots for Rachel from the time he met her pretty little ass when we were in sixth form. I didn't hang with you all back then, but I noticed. She was one hot woman. I can remember clearly what she looked like. She always refused to go out with me. I couldn't believe she turned me down. Of course, that was before I became a changed man."

"I can't believe you're talking about me as if I'm not here."

"George, my boy, that's why we're doing it now. You can't be saying that we're talking about you behind your back," Shayne reasoned.

"So, tell me about the beautiful Rachel," Kyle urged. "Is she looking old since she got married to that old man? You're aware that some people believe that married couples start looking like each other after a while." Everyone laughed.

All eyes turned to George, waiting for his reply.

They were really pathetic, but he loved them, so he'd put them out of their misery.

"Kyle, I'm sure Troy and Shayne can tell you about her since they visited her at the hospital. She hasn't changed much. Still as beautiful as sin. I should say more beautiful. She has matured. Definitely. Breasts a lot fuller. She's filled out in all the right places. Nice curves. She's taller, but that may be because she wears heels now."

"Her height has never bothered you before. Didn't stop you from making love to her all summer of..." Troy injected.

"No need for a trip down memory lane," George interrupted. "I'm dealing with enough as it is. So no trying to titillate me with memories."

"You still in love with her?" The question came clear and unexpected. *Trust Shayne to put him on the spot.*

"Of course not," he blurted out, raising his hands in defiance. "How could I still love her after she went and married that old man?"

"But what did you want her to do? Wait until you decided it was time for you to get married? I think she did the right thing in dumping your ass. And if you want her back, I hope she doesn't make it easy," Troy stated.

"And here I was thinking I'm your friend."

"I am your friend. That's why I'm telling you that what you did those years ago was nonsense. At least you've partially made up for it since she was attacked."

"Sir George, the knight in shining armor, saved the damsel in distress," teased Troy, wielding an imaginary sword with dramatic flair.

"I think we need to eat now, boys. I rest my case. I may be the lawyer, but I can't win anything against you." George raised his hands in surrender. "However, let me make it quite clear—there is nothing that will change my mind about Rachel."

At the appearance of the waitress, the conversation

ended. Having the order prepared in advance had been a sensible thing.

While placing the plates on the table, the pretty young waitress chatted with them briefly, then told them to enjoy the meal and left.

For a while they ate in silence, savoring their plates of barbeque ribs.

George broke the silence.

"I'm always amused when each of you criticizes my lifestyle because you want me to end up like you. You're no fun anymore. I remember when fun was all we cared about. I'm the only one not married yet. But since I have no intention of losing control of my life, I'll probably end up pleasuring all the little old ladies in the retirement home."

"You always say that, but I know you, George. We know you. You're going to end up married, just like we are. I'm going to bet you on it."

"Here, here," Kyle added. "You may think we're all getting boring, but my joy comes from knowing that I have a wife who loves me with every fiber in her bones. The three of you mean everything to me, but having Tamara in my life just makes everything perfect."

For a moment there was silence.

Shayne spoke first. "Kyle, you must be getting ready to counsel George. Man, that was deep."

They all laughed, easing the heavy tension.

"Anyone ready for dessert?" Shayne asked.

"I really shouldn't, but I can't resist the apple pie," Kyle replied.

"Banana split for me," George added.

"I'm going to pass," Shayne grumbled. "Carla has

been complaining about the little bit of growth around my waist. I started back at the gym last week."

"You need to come join us for cricket on Saturdays," George remarked.

"Sorry, that's my day with Darius. I can go to the gym any time I want, but I have to be there for Darius. He's all into the theater group he joined. I saw a presentation the group did a few weeks ago and he's quite good."

"And we didn't know about it. Why didn't we get an invitation?" George asked.

"He thought you wouldn't be interested since it's the theater. He knows how much you're all into cricket."

"I'm going to have to have a chat with that boy. We're culturally appreciative, aren't we?" George asked mockingly.

"Not a bone in any of your bodies," Shayne stated. "I can't remember any of us going to a play."

"I go to the cinema!" Troy exclaimed.

"That doesn't count, Troy. Everyone goes to the cinema."

"Okay, then. I'll be going to his next performance," he promised.

"Me too," Kyle said firmly. "That's what godfathers are for. Support."

At the same time, Shayne's cell phone rang. He pulled it from his pocket and answered, aware of three pairs of eyes on him.

He ended the call. "Well, buddies. I have to go. My mathematically challenged son wants some help with his homework. He's been waiting patiently."

"Shayne, it's Friday!" George exclaimed.

"Yeah, but he likes to do his homework on Fridays so

he doesn't have anything to do on Saturday and Sunday. Of course, I'm always glad when he does this. On Sundays, he always ends up doing some additional studies."

Troy glanced down at his watch too. "I think I better be heading out too. My wife seems to need my loving each night. I'm not complaining, but she hasn't given me any rest since we came back from our honeymoon."

"Sorry, George. Since Shayne is leaving, I'm going to have to desert you too," Kyle said. "But I'm finishing up my latest book, so at least I'll be able to do a bit of writing tonight."

"No worries. I came with Troy. Next bestseller?"

"Hopefully, but it's not fiction. It's more autobiographical and hopefully a book that can help individuals who are blind."

"Sounds good. You know you have our support."

"Thanks, as always," Kyle replied.

"Well, it's time to go," Shayne said, glancing at his watch again.

Troy turned to George. "I'll drop you at the mechanic so you can pick your car up."

Fifteen minutes later, George nodded as Troy drove away. He paid the mechanic and got into his car, but the thought of going directly home to an empty house had lost its appeal.

He drove westward, heading toward the Grantley Adams International Airport. A drive along the east coast would take him about an hour, but he felt the need to spend some time in reflection.

He'd enjoyed the night with his friends, but their talk about love and family had affected him more deeply than he was willing to admit. He loved his friends, but in the past few years his desire to be around them, especially at their homes, had diminished. It always made him feel lonely.

Hanging out with them in a bar or restaurant wasn't a problem. It was at Christmas and birthday dinners when all the families were present that left him feeling this way.

Anger, hot and boiling, rose to the surface. He could be like them now. In fact, he could have been the first to get married. Today, he'd probably have the four children he and Rachel had planned and still have his career. Whenever he looked back he couldn't believe he had let her go. It hadn't really been about the dedication to his work but because he'd been afraid.

He'd been afraid that he wouldn't ever be ready to be a husband or father. He'd been afraid he would not live up to Rachel's expectations of him.

Despite his virility, the slight niggling about his height would surface, but one of his "friends" would lavish him with attention and affection and he would bury those insecurities for a while. Until Rachel had come along and left him feeling vulnerable and helpless.

When he reached the dense vegetation of the East Coast Road, he parked the car on the shoulder and stepped out. Locking the car, he maneuvered between the thick sea-grape shrubs, reaching the soft sand of the beach.

The ocean lay asleep, an unusual occurrence for this part of the island, known for its restlessness.

He stripped his clothes off and dropped them on the sand, the cool ocean breeze caressing him softly.

He felt wild and free, at one with nature. He stretched his hands skyward, embracing the tranquility of the night. Picking his clothes up, he strolled down the beach, stopping when he reached a curve in the shoreline. He turned around and headed back to the car, sure to put his clothes back on before he left the beach.

The drive back to St. George, the parish where he lived, took less time than his trip there, but he felt much better.

Entering the house, he went directly to his bedroom, stripped his clothes off for the second time and headed to the shower.

Five minutes later, he was lying in bed, his body and spirit feeling better than it had in weeks. He had tried to clear his mind of the things that were troubling him and had come to the realization that he needed Rachel back in his life.

He didn't know how he was going to prove to her that he was a changed man, that his priorities were changing, but he would do whatever was needed to let her know. He planned on helping her to realize that he was the man for her. It would take time and effort on his part, but he wanted what Shayne and Kyle and Troy had. Not only the idea of family, but also he wanted his face to light up, like theirs did, when he talked about his love ones.

He gripped the pillow on his bed and pretended it was Rachel, like he'd done many times when he was a teenager.

Inside he felt warm and cozy. He smiled in the darkness. He was getting all romantic and vulnerable.

He still loved her…loved her with an intensity that he didn't know was possible.

He smiled again.

Tomorrow always held promise and possibilities.

He just hoped it was not too late for him. Though he'd defied his destiny many years ago, he hoped that fate was still smiling down on him.

Chapter 8

Rachel closed the door behind her, thinking she might take a nap, but she could not sleep. The pain wasn't all that bad, so she couldn't understand why she couldn't sleep. Sleep hadn't come easily since the attack. Each time she closed her eyes she would relive that day. She'd never been one to wallow in affliction, so her response in this case worried her. It was so totally out of character.

Walking over to the window, she watched Gregory and Jonathan playing cricket. She'd been so glad there was a boy her son's age next door. At first, Gregory had not been happy when she'd told him they were returning to Barbados. But he'd accepted her decision without throwing a tantrum. In fact, her son never threw tantrums. He was the model son, something that worried her a bit. She loved Gregory but he was too introspective, a bit too quiet and serious. She wanted her son to live life to the fullest; she wanted him to have fun. Edward's parenting had been a bit too much like her father's. Too much work and too little play make Jack a dull boy. Gregory had had very little play.

Outside, Gregory took the bat and stood in front of the makeshift wickets. In the past few weeks, she'd seen him playing more and more cricket. He was his father's child. The usual ache she felt whenever she thought of George sharpened until she felt the familiar sting of tears.

Jonathan bowled the ball and Gregory stuck it powerfully across the lawn until it came to rest in the garden next door.

The memories were strong. She saw George holding the bat in his hand, his muscular body graceful as he stroked the ball.

Gregory looked in the direction of the house and, seeing her, he waved.

She returned the greeting and watched as he prepared for the next ball. The sound of the phone ringing interrupted her thoughts, and she turned instinctively to answer it. Pain stabbed her in the side and she doubled over with the impact of it. She straightened slowly and groaned when the ringing stopped. When she reached it, she looked down.

Unknown name. Unknown number.

There was nothing she could do about it. If it was important, the caller would try again.

She walked toward the sofa, taking the handset with her in case it rang again.

She eased herself onto the chair, reaching for the magazine she'd been reading. She'd always loved this room. It was here she'd spent most of her time with her father. She missed him even more now that she was home because photos and other reminders of him remained.

She glanced at a photo she wished she could move. It was one of her father and George. She tried each day to keep her eyes off it, but she couldn't help it. Her gaze would inevitably linger before she looked away.

The room had not changed much since her childhood. It had always been homey, a sanctuary. Flowers continued to bloom in crystal vases her mother had collected over the years. Her mother could tell visitors the story behind each vase and where she had purchased it. Her parents had loved to travel and each of the vases represented one of their trips.

Her mother and father had married when very young, but she'd only come along when both of them were in their later thirties. Her father had died exactly twenty-two years after she was born. Her birthdays were always tinged with a bit of sadness. But at least he had seen her complete her secondary education. He'd been delighted when she had been accepted at Oxford University.

Her memories of her father were good ones. He'd been the perfect husband and father. He'd loved her mother unconditionally. A soft-spoken, gentle man, he had been a voracious reader, enjoying anything from fiction to nonfiction to poetry. He would read any poet, but he'd adored the romantic work of English poet John Keats and the poetry of protest of Guyanese poet Martin Carter. Complete opposite in style and content, but that's the kind of man her father was and she'd loved him. She'd been his "Bright Star," a nickname her mother still used on occasions.

At times like these she missed him. She had used her father's death to motivate her to study harder. When she received her law degree, she had taken it to the cemetery where he was buried and showed it to him.

The shrill sound of the phone dragged her from the past. She answered, wondering if it was her mother.

No. George.

Why was he calling?

"Rachel, this is George," he said. His voice was low and husky. "I called to find out how you were doing. Troy told me that you had been discharged."

"I'm doing fine. I should have called to let you know. I'm not sure when I'll be cleared to go back to work, but when I see the doctor next week, he'll let me know."

"Has the pain eased up?" he asked politely.

Why was he being so nice to her? She didn't want him to be nice to her. When he was like this, she ached for him.

"A bit. I still have to use the painkillers at times, but most of the time it's bearable."

"Well, I'm glad you're okay. Please say hello to your mom for me. I'll see if I can drop by sometime."

"No!" she shouted. Immediately, she regretted her sharp response. She had to act normally. He could never find out what was wrong.

"I'm sorry I asked," he said. "You have a good night and take care."

The soft click of the phone told her he was gone.

He was angry. She had hurt him again.

She didn't have to be so mean to him. He didn't deserve her attitude. All he'd been to her since she returned home had been polite. He'd been the perfect gentleman and all she'd done was hurt him. She knew she'd hurt him.

She glanced at the clock. It was almost six o'clock. Gregory needed to come in and take his shower before he did his homework and then have dinner. He had school tomorrow. She couldn't believe the weekend had gone by so quickly.

As if by clockwork, she heard the door open and Gregory rushed into the room, his face animated with his excitement.

She rose, listening intently as he described how he'd hit six runs and sent the ball sailing over the rooftop to the other side of the house. He held up the ball as if it could show her the punishment it had received.

"You've got to take your bath. Your grandmother is soon going to be home, and you know she wants us to eat with her."

"I'll be done in a flash, Mom."

"Good, and don't forget behind the ears."

"Yes, Mom," he groaned.

He raced upstairs and left her there. Maybe for the next few moments she wouldn't have to think of George.

She'd focus all of her attention on the person who loved her most in the world.

Her son.

Halfway across the island, George slammed the phone down. Damn, he hated outward displays of anger. He always tried to control his ire. His body's mass rippled with bulging muscles and he knew his strength and ability. He could, if he wanted to, crack a man's hand with his bare fist, not that he'd ever do that.

He closed his eyes, breathing in deeply.

He had to ignore her attitude. She seemed intent on riling him up but he would not give her the satisfaction of seeing him lose control. He suspected that she'd use it to discredit him if the opportunity ever arose.

However, he had no intentions of letting her deter him from his plan to win her back.

Tomorrow was Monday, another day, another possibility. Her attitude tonight was only a minor setback.

Nothing would stop him from accomplishing his goal.

Nothing.

Chapter 9

Morning came with its startling, tropical beauty. Outside, the pale gray of the early dawn morphed into bright orange and red before settling into the brilliant blue of daytime.

Rachel stumbled up the driveway and stopped when she reached the steps of the verandah.

Her breath came in ragged, labored sounds. The niggling of pain in her side had worsened. Her attempt to take a short walk had seemed a good idea, but she had pushed herself too much.

Last night she had been unable to sleep. She'd tossed and turned and tossed some more until finally slipping into a restless sleep. She had awakened just before five o'clock, deciding to venture outdoors for a short, brisk walk. She missed her daily morning run, but since the doctor had recommended only light exercises, a short walk seemed reasonable.

A week had passed since she'd last spoken to George, yet she could not forget the fact that she'd been so mean to him. She'd been challenged by a desire to do the right thing.

On her walk, she'd decided that she'd tell George about their son. She only hoped that the inevitable anger would be replaced by joy to know him.

Rachel took the key from her pocket and unlocked the door. The sound of the television greeted her. Gregory was already up. From the direction of the kitchen, the piquant aroma of freshly brewed coffee titillated her nostrils.

She headed to her room. She'd take her bath and then come back for breakfast. She was hungry and her mother's promise of fluffy bakes and codfish cakes had tickled her taste buds. She had been requesting the local breakfast delicacies since her return to the island.

Five minutes later, feeling totally refreshed, she entered the kitchen, clad in a tube top and shorts. She could get accustomed to this life of leisure, but in a week, said the doctor, she should be able to return to work, if she promised to take it easy. This morning she had already broken her promise.

A part of her missed the energy of the prosecutor's office, but catching up on her pile of novels and watching some of her favorite movies on AMC was enough to send her searching for a rich man to take care of her.

When she entered the kitchen, Gregory was already there, his plate stacked with his codfish cakes and bakes.

"Good morning," she greeted Grace cheerfully then turned to her son. "Gregory, you're not going to eat all those pancakes, are you? You're going to have a stomachache if you eat so many."

"Grandma says I can leave two of them to eat later when I'm hungry. She said that my stomach must have a maw worm."

"If you're not careful you'll blow up to the size of a whale," she replied, stretching her hands wide apart to show him the size.

He giggled.

"Let the boy eat what he wants," Grace said, chuckling. "He's a growing boy. He'll burn that off in a couple of hours. You sit and let me fill your plate. You know you're no better when it comes to pancakes. He's just like you in that respect. When you were young, you ate like a horse too. I kept wondering if *you* would even slow down."

"Yeah, that's why I was so chubby when I entered high school. Luckily, I realized that I had to moderate things and get some exercise."

"How was your walk? I would have loved to come, but I really can't get up at that godforsaken hour. I need my beauty sleep—unless there are some eligible aging bachelors walking too."

"Mom, behave yourself!"

"I assure you I am, but that doesn't mean that blood isn't still flowing through my veins. I may be getting old but I'm not dead."

"Mom!" Rachel admonished again, glancing in Gregory's direction.

"He's a big boy. I am sure he knows more about the facts of life than you think."

Gregory was grinning from ear to ear.

Oh my God, she thought. Her son was growing up

right before her and she didn't even realize it. How on Earth was she going to explain the facts of life and his raging hormones to him? His father would be able to tell him all he needed to know.

"Okay, I understand, Mom," Rachel said, continuing to stare at her son curiously.

Like his father, he was not going to be too tall, but already his body was developing the same kind of physique.

"Anything planned for the day, Gregory?"

"Not really, Mom. Can Jonathan hang out here today and play video games? We have a project we have to work on too."

"That's fine. As long as your grandmother says it's okay, I'll call Marjorie."

"It's fine with me," Grace consented. "I won't be here for most of the morning, but I'll bring in pizza for the boys and Chinese for us from this wonderful new restaurant that opened last week. Marjorie told me the food is divine."

"That settles it. I'll call Marjorie as soon as I finish breakfast," Rachel replied.

Rachel picked up two of the pancakes from the platter. Today was going to be a good day. She planned on spending the day reading and watching television.

Later tonight she would decide how and when she would tell George about his son.

George cleared his desk and placed the files he wanted to work on that night in his briefcase. Although it was Saturday, he'd come into the office to work on the final preparations for a trial that would be starting on Monday. He'd worked all morning and was ready to head home.

But before he did he planned on making a stop to visit Rachel's mother. He knew he should call Mrs. Davis first but suspected that Rachel would not approve. Rachel would continue to keep him at arm's length, but he had no intention of allowing her barriers to remain standing. Tonight, at least, she would have no choice but to invite him in.

Ten minutes later he was driving toward the parish of Christ Church where she lived.

He'd always loved her home and quiet neighborhood, which contrasted with the noisy village where he'd grown up. He had long left the village life, and Rachel's home had always made him aspire to have that type of house. He hoped his aspirations hadn't made him into a snob, but he enjoyed the comforts of his current lifestyle.

The truth was…he wanted to see Rachel. His workload had increased so much in the past week he'd tried to push her to the back of his mind. It was the only way he could focus on his cases. Not that his attempt had been totally successful. Rachel's image had an uncanny way of reappearing when he least expected it to.

As he neared Rachel's district, he experienced a moment of trepidation and wondered if he should turn back. Was he trying to make something out of nothing? Something buried in the past that should stay there?

Despite his reasoning, his car seemed to have a will of its own, and he turned onto the street flanked by two massive royal palms.

Memories of the joyous days he had spent there came rushing back. Here, under the canopy of a mahogany tree, he'd kissed Rachel for the first time. He'd kissed her with a fervor he'd not experienced before. He had whispered "I love you" as the moon's rays had caressed them tenderly.

As his car drew nearer to her house, he saw two boys playing outside. One of the boys was batting while the other had made his run-up and was about to bowl the ball.

The batsman struck the ball and it flew into the air, going a long way across the wide lawn before it landed just where he'd stopped his car.

He stepped out of the car, reached down and picked up the ball before the bowler could retrieve it.

He wondered who the boys were but assumed they were the sons of residents, even though the batsman seemed oddly familiar.

"Thanks for getting our ball, mister," the batsman said politely, putting his hand out as if to challenge him.

He handed the ball over, admiring the boy's spunk. He liked how he looked at him, his stare unwavering.

"Who you looking for, mister?" the other boy asked.

"I'm looking for Grace Davis. She lives here."

"She isn't at home right now," he responded.

"What about her daughter?"

"She's not feeling well and she's sleeping. You want me to wake her up?" the batsman asked. Who was this boy? George wondered.

"No, that's fine. I'll call back later. Thanks for your information." He moved to walk away and then turned back.

"Can I ask your names?"

"You can," the batsman replied but did not provide them. George shrugged, but then the boy answered.

"I'm Gregory and this is my best friend, Jonathan. Rachel Davis is my mom."

George felt the color drain from his face.

"How old are you, son?" he asked.

"Why do you want to know?" Gregory challenged.

"Just curious," he replied.

"Twelve."

George turned away without another word but stopped and searched in his pocket, eventually finding one of his business cards in his wallet.

He handed it to Gregory. "Give this to your mother for me."

"No problem" was the reply.

He didn't know how he got into the car, didn't know how he got home, but in the quiet of his house, strange, crazy thoughts crowded his mind.

The questions hovered at the edge of his consciousness, but he didn't give them completeness…not until he pulled out an album of photos of himself from a storage box he kept in a drawer in his office.

As he held the album, his hands trembled.

He slipped the cover open, his eyes searching hungrily for the photos. There were none on the first page, but a few pages forward the image he sought confirmed his suspicions.

The boy in the photo staring back at him was almost the spitting image of the boy he had seen.

Was Gregory his son?

A stupid question. The evidence was right there before him.

George stifled the urge to get up and drive back over there.

During the next few hours a range of emotions

washed over him. Anger, acceptance, then fear. How the hell was he going to handle this? He had a son. He knew nothing about being a father.

He wasn't even sure what Rachel's reaction would be. What if the boy didn't like him? He could force her to let him see Gregory. He could have a DNA test, prove that Gregory was his son.

But then what?

What he'd seen today explained her reactions to him. The times she'd refused his offer to visit her mother. The reluctance to be his friend.

Her deceit answered all of his questions.

He picked up the phone and called Troy. Of the three friends, George was always the calm, controlled one, but this evening he felt different.

Troy answered the phone on the first ring.

"What's up, man?" Troy greeted.

"Are you busy, Troy? Can you pass by here sometime today? I have something important to discuss with you."

"Sure, I'm leaving work in an hour or so. I'll come right over. Have any food?"

"Yeah, I'll cook something. What do you feel like eating? Pasta?"

"Now, how did I know that would be it? Boy, you need to learn how to cook other things. I'll see you in a bit."

He hung the phone up and headed to the kitchen. Maybe cooking would keep his mind off this messed-up situation.

For the next hour, he focused on the task before him. While the saucepans were bubbling furiously away, he showered quickly and returned downstairs to add the finishing touches. He couldn't cook most stuff, but he loved pasta and there were enough varieties of the product and different recipes to keep his palate happy. He'd picked up quite a few recipes on the Food Network.

Troy arrived about two hours later. By then the meal was done, minus the few mouthfuls he'd eaten.

"I hope what we have to talk about can wait until I've finished eating."

"We can talk while we eat."

"I prefer to eat. I'm so hungry. I was so glad when you called and offered dinner. Sandra and the kids went to spend the evening at Tamara's, along with Carla and her kids. A girls' night out, I was told. I always imagine them talking about our abilities in bed."

When George didn't laugh, he paused briefly, then said, "I think we better talk about this thing that's bothering you while we eat."

"I think I have a son," he said without hesitation.

"Shit," Troy replied. "Okay, I expected something big, but not so humongous."

"His name is Gregory. He's twelve and he looks just like me," he said.

"Rachel?" Troy asked.

"Yes. She had my son and didn't even tell me."

"When did you find out?"

"I went over to Rachel's home this evening. Her mother was out and Rachel was taking a rest. The boy was playing cricket outside." He opened the album on the table. "See that photo? He looks just like me."

"Holy shit!" Troy exclaimed. "This is amazing. What are you going to do?"

"Going to do? That's why I called you over here. I don't have a clue what to do. I have to claim him. He's my son, but how on Earth am I going to father a kid? I don't know a thing about fatherhood."

"Okay, okay, let's eat and calm down. We'll talk rationally about this. You're going to have to talk to Rachel. Let her know that you know."

George snorted.

"You could just leave things as they are," Troy suggested.

"I can't do that. I can't just pretend that he doesn't exist. Just because she hasn't put me on any birth certificate doesn't make him any less mine."

"I am here to support you in any way you want. But talk to her, George. I know it's not going to be easy. Maybe she plans on telling you. I don't think she would expect you not to see him. The island is too small. Meeting him would be inevitable."

"But how could she do this to me? He's twelve years old," George said, slamming his hand on the table.

"I know Rachel. There is more to this. Maybe she found out just after she left the island. There are so many possible explanations. When you broke up with her, you made it clear you didn't want any commitment—that you wanted to focus on the job."

"But I should have been told. He's my son. She has denied me almost thirteen years of his life. How am I expected to feel?"

"I will say this—at least you have the rest of your life with him. What if she had not come back? You'd have never known."

George went silent. He was too confused, too emotional about this.

"Thanks for the advice. By tomorrow I'll be fine. It's just the shock of seeing my son for the first time.

I wasn't prepared for it. Boy, if I had a weak heart, I would have expired right there," he said, laughing drily.

"At least you didn't. You sure you don't want me to stay for the night? I'm sure Sandra won't mind."

"No, I'll be fine. I just need to sleep this off."

"And promise me you won't do anything rash or silly. Just look at this as a blessing. You have a son. Each of you is going to have to deal with this situation maturely. The only feelings you should be concerned about are his."

"That's true," George said passively. "Thanks for stopping by, bro."

Troy stood to leave, and George followed him. At the front door, Troy gave him a strong bear hug. "Everything is going to be fine. Just take each day one step at a time."

George nodded and watched as his best friend walked away. When the car disappeared down the driveway he returned to the kitchen. He washed the dishes and headed for his room.

A quick shower later, he was in bed, his Kindle opened to the latest Patterson.

Reading always seemed to calm him. For now, he just wanted to clear his mind of his troubles. Tomorrow would be another day. Tomorrow, he knew they'd have to talk.

"Mom, I forgot to tell Grandma that some man, a friend of hers, dropped by today while she was out. You were sleeping so I didn't wake you."

"He came to the door?"

"No, we were…outside playing cricket," he mumbled.

"Gregory, I thought I told you not to go outside in the sun so early. You promised me."

"I'm sorry, Mom, but outside was perfect for a good knock."

"But you disobeyed me. We'll talk about this later. I'll tell you how long you're grounded for."

"Aw, Mom," he whined.

"Don't you 'aw, Mom' me! I have one rule. Obey me. You tell me about this man. Did he leave his name?"

"I'm not sure, but I had this strange feeling like I know him. Oh, he did give me his business card. It's in my pocket." He pulled it out and handed it to her.

Rachel grew pale. It was George. His message was clear. He knew. Damn it, he knew.

"Mom, what's wrong?" Gregory asked.

"Nothing, honey. I'll be fine."

"You want me to bring you a glass of water?" he asked.

"Yes, thank you."

She sat while he went to the kitchen and filled a glass.

She had known it was inevitable, but she'd not expected it to come so soon. She was surprised he hadn't called, but then she realized this was George. He'd deal with his anger and then he'd call. He had to be in control. That was the George she knew.

So for now this would be a waiting game. He'd call when he was ready.

Until he did, she would have to wonder what approach he'd take. What would be the consequences of her deceit?

She took the glass from Gregory and downed it,

wishing it were something a lot stronger. She needed something strong to calm her nerves.

"Are you feeling better?" Gregory asked.

"I'm better. Just a slight dizzy spell. Nothing to worry about. You go up to your room and take a shower. I expect lights out by nine."

"Yes, Mom. And I'm sorry I disobeyed you."

"Okay, you run on up." She pulled him to her, kissing him on his cheek. He hugged her. She wondered how much longer his displays of affection would continue. He was getting older. Those kisses would probably end while he battled with his masculinity and peer pressure.

She stood finally and took her time cleaning the kitchen, making sure she left everything spick-and-span.

She walked to her room. Tonight would be a long night, but it was the thought of tomorrow that she dreaded more.

Chapter 10

In contrast to the previous day, Sunday morning brought misty showers.

Rachel frowned but immediately stopped. She didn't want to encourage furrows on her forehead. She stretched, attempting to work the wariness from her body. She groaned, the slight ache in her side a reminder of her walk the day before.

She'd wanted to go walking again this morning, but dark clouds in the east, a promise of rain, had deterred her from leaving.

There was a knock on the door and her mother entered.

"Good morning, honey. How are you feeling this morning?"

"Fine, Mom."

"Why the gloomy face? I hope the rain is not already

having an effect on you." Her mother smiled encouragingly.

"He knows, Mom," she blurted out.

"Who knows? Knows what? What are you taking about, child?"

"George knows. He came by to visit you yesterday. You weren't here and I was asleep. He saw Gregory."

"He would be a fool not to realize Gregory was his. What are you going to do? Call him?"

"I think that may be the best thing to do. I had made up my mind just the other day to let him know. He must be so angry."

"What man wouldn't be? He has a twelve-year-old son. What did you expect? Smiles? Immediate forgiveness? I warned you this was going to happen."

"I don't want to lose my son."

"I'm sure you won't. The George I know would be angry for a while, but he won't take Gregory away from you. He may want joint custody."

"Joint custody?" she asked, but she knew that it was a strong possibility. A possibility she dreaded.

"Rachel, you have to accept the inevitable. George will want to see his son."

She shrugged. What her mother said was true. She only hoped he'd give Gregory time to adjust to the truth. She'd have to talk to Gregory. She just hoped he wouldn't hate her for her deception.

At that moment, the phone rang. It was George. She was sure of it.

Her mother answered and indicated that the call was for her.

She took it, glad when her mother left the room.

"Yes, this is Rachel," she said. Her voice sounded strange. It didn't seem like hers.

"We have to talk," he said. His voice was calm, controlled.

"Okay."

"When is good for you?"

"Tomorrow evening."

"Your home?"

"No, somewhere neutral."

"Okay, I'll call in the morning, but I'll pick you up some time in the late evening."

He hung up.

Rachel shivered. She could feel the cold. His voice had been distant, expressionless.

She could tell he had no intention of making this easy for her. Maybe she deserved it.

She put the phone down, walked toward the bed and lay down.

When the tears came she could not stop them. She cried and cried until she couldn't anymore.

Exhausted, she fell asleep.

When she woke several hours later, her son was staring down at her.

She smiled. She loved him. He was the one true thing in her life.

"You all right, Mom?"

"I'm fine, Gregory. I'm just a bit tired. Want to come lie with me and talk, maybe watch a movie?"

"We could, but Grandma said we need to come eat lunch. And I'm hungry."

Her stomach grumbled. He laughed.

"Tell her I'll be there in a bit. You've finished your homework?"

"Yes."

"Good. You get to choose the movie."

"I know exactly what we're going to watch. *Toy Story 3.*"

"Good choice. Your grandma was waiting until you were ready to watch it. You want to call Jonathan and ask him to come over?"

"Sure, Mom. I'll call him right now."

"He can come for lunch if his mother doesn't mind. I'm sure your grandmother cooked enough."

"I'll tell him."

Rachel watched as Gregory raced out of the room. Didn't he ever get tired? He was changing. He was slowly adapting to being on the island. Finding a good friend next door had helped. Jonathan was a good boy and she was glad for that.

In the bathroom, she washed her face and went downstairs.

Having an afternoon of television and fun with her mother and son was a great way to deal with what was going on in her life.

Tomorrow would come soon, but for now she tried to forget the impending meeting with George.

George visited his mother each Sunday morning, but it was something he hated doing. She no longer knew him. He still felt guilty at placing her here at the home, but reasoning from Shayne and Troy had made him realize that he didn't have the qualifications or the know-how to take care of her. He'd watched his mother deteriorate from the vibrant hardworking single mother she'd been to a woman who didn't even know her son.

When he walked into her room, she was sitting in her usual chair. Physically, his mother had not aged much. She was still the beautiful woman he remembered. His mother had been the perfect wife and housewife. She reminded him of Bree on *Desperate Housewives*. She always had to be perfectly courteous and she could never be caught outside without wearing immaculately applied makeup. Even now.

He knew it was silly, but he paid for her to be taken to have her hair and nails done each week. He didn't care. He wanted her to be happy, even if she no longer knew what happiness was.

She looked up when she realized he was there, her eyes sparkling like midnight stars.

"Oh, hi. I'm Sylvia. It's so nice of you to come visit me. My son came yesterday. He's coming again in a day or two. Come and sit with me. Let me tell you about my son." She laughed and clapped her hands.

He walked over, bending to place a kiss on her cheek before sitting. She raised her hand and rested it lightly against his cheek. "My son kisses me just like that," she said. "He's such a sweet boy, you know. He's a lawyer. The best lawyer."

"I'm sure he misses you."

"He does…but he's married to the sweetest girl. Her name is… What's her name? I can't remember, but she's pretty, really pretty, and has a kind heart. She's going to be a lawyer too, but she's in Britain, or is it France? I can't remember things sometimes."

"That's fine. I don't remember things sometimes either."

"You're such a nice boy, too. You remind me of my son. He's a good boy. I love him."

He took her hand in his. "I'm sure he knows you love him."

"I hope so. I'm feeling tired now. I need to lie down. You can come see me again. My name is Sylvia."

When she stood, he took her hand and helped her to the bed.

She looked up at him with the most innocent of eyes.

"I have to kneel and say my prayers before I go to sleep. You can pray with me. I don't always remember my prayers, so I just kneel sometimes."

"Then I'll pray for you tonight."

He helped her to her knees and then joined her.

The words of the childhood prayers they said together so many years ago came to mind.

"In the little bed I lie, Heavenly Father, hear my cry...."

By the time he reached the end, tears trickled down his cheeks.

He helped her up and back to the bed. She turned to look at him.

"There is no need to cry, son. Everything is going to be all right."

When she was tucked in, she closed her eyes and soon drifted off to sleep, a happy look on her face.

For a while he stood watching her sleep, his memories of a better time increasing his ache for the time when he didn't have a care in the world.

He glanced down at his watch and realized it was getting late. He'd promised Rachel he'd pick her up by six o'clock. He had about twenty minutes to get over there.

* * *

That evening, when George pulled up outside Rachel's home, she was sitting on the patio. She stood but did not move. She seemed reluctant to join him, but eventually she walked toward the car. He got out, walked around the car and opened the door for her, waiting until she was seated before closing the door and returning to his seat.

He strapped his seat belt on and turned to her.

"How are you feeling? The wound is healing well?" he asked politely.

"Yes, I get a bit of pain sometimes, but it's getting better," she replied primly. He noticed she sat closer to the door.

She hesitated briefly and then added, "Can we dispel with the pleasantries and get to the purpose of this meeting?"

"I would prefer to wait until we get where I'm taking you before we talk."

"I didn't think we needed to. We can just talk while we drive?" she suggested.

"But you're really in no position to negotiate," he stated. "It's either we do things my way or we do it in court."

She didn't say anything. His words were clear. She didn't have a choice.

For the rest of the drive, there was silence, the stiff tension in her posture evidence of her disapproval.

He drove along the south coast, heading toward the city of Bridgetown, turning into the driveway of Bert's Bar & Restaurant.

"My favorite restaurant. You'll love it."

He wondered if he was going about this the right

way. The expression on her face told him that she didn't much care.

He was still angry, but during the night he'd thought long and hard about their past. To be honest, he was still not totally sure what his course of action would be, but he felt that she deserved a chance to explain what she had done.

He'd dumped her like a hot potato and she would have had to make a decision on her own. He wasn't even sure that if she had told him, he might not have recommended an abortion.

It wasn't usual for him to come here to Bert's on a Sunday night and this contrasting quietness with the noisy atmosphere he'd experienced on Friday was an interesting one.

A waitress greeted them immediately and led them into the interior.

When they were seated, she left them with the menus to peruse.

Rachel glanced briefly at the menu and put it back on the table.

"The ribs are to die for," he said.

"I'd prefer not to eat," she replied abruptly.

"You can't refuse to sample the ribs."

She hesitated briefly, then said, "I guess I can try them."

"Good, that's my girl," he said, motioning to the waitress, who was looking in their direction. After he placed the order, he sat back in the chair, allowing his gaze to linger on her.

He noticed her shiver, but the stubborn look on her face remained.

"So why didn't you tell me, Rachel? How could you

keep my son from me?" he finally asked as he leaned forward and placed his elbows on the table.

"I think you already know the answers to those questions," she replied calmly. "Why indeed?" She laughed cynically. "Maybe it's because I was just about to start my career and hopefully marry the man I loved, only to discover that he didn't love or want me anymore. What was I supposed to do?"

"You could have come to me, told me," he suggested after a slight pause.

"After you made it quite clear I was a burden, that the only way you would succeed was if we broke up? When I discovered I was pregnant, I wondered if I should tell you, but you'd already moved on. Who was I to burden you with something you had made it quite clear you didn't want in your life then?" He could tell his questions had annoyed her. Her eyes flashed with anger.

"We could argue all around the world, but I can't agree with you," he stated bluntly.

"So you tell me where you want to go from here."

He didn't blink. "I want to know my son."

"I suspected that would be your answer. But let me make this clear. You hurt my son in the process, you'll have to answer to me."

"That's no fault of mine," he retorted. "You allowed it to happen."

"See, it's all about blame?" she said bitterly. "I did what I thought was right back when you did what you thought was right for you. Now, you want to do what's right for you without the consequences of your actions. I pray for your sake that Gregory wants you in his life."

"I'm sorry," he said quietly, his anger deflating. He

paused. "Fine, we'll do it your way. Just don't deny me my son," he pleaded.

"Let's hold off letting him know for a few weeks until he gets accustomed to having you around. It will mean a certain level of intimacy between us, but I am willing to do this for Gregory."

"I would like to tell him now, but your reasoning makes sense. So we have an agreement?"

"Yes," she replied.

At the same time, the waitress reappeared, her hands laden with the two plates of ribs.

The honeyed scent of the barbequed ribs wafted in the air.

His mouth watered in anticipation.

As she placed everything on the table, he stared at Rachel. She was even more beautiful than she'd been thirteen years ago. She reminded him of a young Vanessa Williams—that slight interracial look, her eyes an unusual shade of brown. He'd always loved her eyes—and knew them well. He'd seen them flash with anger, pained with sadness and flaming with desire. In those days her eyes had been true to the maxim *the eyes are the windows to the soul,* and he had seen her soul. Unfortunately, he'd not let her into his.

When the waitress left with an "Enjoy your meal," he continued to watch Rachel surreptitiously. She ate with gusto, like she always had. Not one to pick at the food on her plate, she savored each bite with relish.

When she took a succulent rib on a fork and drew it to her mouth, his arousal was spontaneous. She nibbled it neatly, but the red sauce smeared her lips. Her tongue flicked out, licking the sauce. He watched her tongue, remembered the things she had done to him with it. His body shuddered with the memory.

She stopped midbite and looked at him, realized he was not eating.

"What's the problem?" she asked nervously. "Why are you staring at me like that?"

"Sorry, didn't mean to stare. Finish your meal," he replied, taking a rib.

They ate in silence, each savoring the meal but still aware of each other.

When George was done, he placed his utensils on the plate and leaned back in the chair. Rachel looked up.

George's gaze continued to linger. "You are more beautiful than you were as a teenager," he finally said when she placed her fork on her plate. "You've blossomed into a stunner. Anguilla must have been good for you."

"I liked it there. The slow pace, the quietness of the island, but I didn't like feeling as if I was cut off from Barbados."

"Was it easy to readjust to being back?" he asked, curiosity getting the better of him.

"Not really. In some ways Anguilla is a lot like Barbados, but yes, there are definite differences. Anguilla is still very much about family life. Here, it's about modernization, which in itself is not a bad thing, but when most people no longer care about each other, it's sad."

"But you seem to have settled back in quite well."

"I was lucky to get the job." She nodded, smiling briefly. "I'm enjoying it so far. Well, except for one minor incident."

"And you've put that behind you?"

"Yes, I will do the right things. My office is sending me for counseling as soon as I return to work in a week. But I've been advised to take things easy, even when I return. A few of my cases have been reassigned." She glanced at her watch. "I'd better get home."

George signaled to the waitress and a few minutes later she brought the bill. Placing the money between the wallet, he left her the fee and a generous tip.

The drive back to Rachel's house was quiet, each in their own thoughts.

He wondered what she was thinking. For all intents and purposes, things had gone better than he had expected. But maybe his handling of the situation had made things easier to talk about.

The compromise they'd reached made sense. They'd both been mature and rational about the situation.

When the car stopped, he jumped out immediately, going around to the passenger side to make sure she didn't let herself out.

Rachel stepped out, her brow furrowed. "There was no need for you to get out. You aren't coming in."

"What kind of gentleman would I be if I let you walk to the door by yourself?"

"A smart one," came her quick retort.

"Then we would have to conclude that I'm not too smart. You did always outperform me at school and you were a whole year younger."

She smiled, her face softening for the first time that evening.

"It's good to see you smile. You don't smile as often as you used to."

"Those were different days, when I thought I didn't have a care in the world. I had to grow up."

He didn't respond, didn't know what to say. Maybe what she said was true. They'd both grown up.

When they reached the patio, he stopped, watching her walk to the door.

She put the key in the lock and turned to him. "Thanks for being understanding about this situation. I haven't even told you how sorry I am. I did what I thought was best at the time."

She opened the door, but before she entered she turned to him. For a moment time stopped, and they were teenagers again, the memory of their first kiss vivid.

He stepped onto the patio, stopping when he stood before her.

He glanced at her lips. She glanced at his.

He lowered his head, she raised hers.

His lips touched hers tentatively, softly. He groaned, his need to be touched by her making his legs weak.

His placed his hand at the back of her neck and pulled her to him gently, loving the feel of her softness pressed against him.

She tasted like honey, just as he remembered.

His tongue slipped between her lips and into the sweetness. At first he kissed her gently, probing with his tongue, but then he sucked on her tongue hungrily, wanting more of her.

His free hand shifted upward, cupping one firm breast.

And then she pulled away, her breath coming in short, erratic spasms.

"I can't do this," she gasped.

She pushed the door open, leaving him standing

there, his erect penis pressing painfully against his zipper.

He turned around and walked toward his car.

Tonight had been unexpected, but he now knew something. He was as much in love with her today as he had been thirteen years ago.

Chapter 11

By the time Rachel took a shower, Gregory was already in his room. She'd planned on waiting until tomorrow, but then she decided to get it over with.

She knocked on his door and waited until he said to come in. He was a boy and needed some measure of privacy. She didn't want any surprises.

He was sitting on the bed reading. He had a laptop that he used only for schoolwork. He didn't care much for the social aspect of the computer and for that she was glad. However, she did fear the time he'd start asking her about the facts of life. But with George about to step into his life, that wouldn't be too much of a problem.

He rested the book on the bed when she sat.

"What's wrong, Mom?"

"Nothing's wrong, but I need to talk to you about something important."

"What is it?"

She hesitated. She wasn't even sure what to say. She sent a silent word heavenward.

She breathed in deeply.

"It's about the man who came to visit your grandmother yesterday. He had invited me out on a date. Would you have a problem with that?" she asked.

He looked up at her, his eyes wary.

"He likes you?" he asked.

"We're just friends. He was my boyfriend years ago."

"I'm not sure how I feel about it, but I think it'll be okay if you go."

"Thanks, honey. Sometimes he's going to invite you along too."

At that he shrugged. "I guess that's okay too."

"Thanks for understanding," she told him finally.

He closed his book and placed it on the dresser.

"I think I'm going to bed now. I'm tired," he said quietly.

She rose from the bed and bent to kiss him. He placed his arms around her and hugged her tightly.

When he took his arms from around her, he smiled and said, "I love you."

"Love you, honey," she replied.

She left the room and headed downstairs where she knew her mother was waiting.

"So how did it go?" Grace asked.

"It went better than I expected, on both counts."

"What about Gregory?"

"I told him George and I will be going out sometimes. He took it better than I thought. George and I decided that we'll wait until he gets accustomed to having him around before we tell him."

"That may be the best way to deal with this. Gregory will be okay. You send a prayer heavenward later and ask Him to work it out."

"I'll do that, Mom. I think I'm going to go up to bed."

"Your side is okay?"

"Yes, I may have done a bit too much today, but it's not bad. A bit sore."

"You go on up. I'll stay downstairs. I have to call Marjorie. I promised I'd call her back so I know I'm in for a long conversation, but I don't mind. I have some gossip of my own to share."

She walked over to Rachel and kissed her on the cheek.

"Sleep well, honey."

"I'll see you in the morning. And no staying up too late talking on the phone."

"I promise," she replied, smiling.

Rachel left as her mother reached to pick up the phone.

In her room, she stripped, put on a nightie and reached in the top shelf of her cupboards to retrieve the photo album.

She took it down, holding it as if it were some precious treasure.

She sat on the carpet of her room, opening the album.

As she looked at the photos, vivid memories came back as if it were yesterday. She smiled. She'd given George a run for his money. It had taken him weeks for her to agree to go out with him, but she'd enjoyed the courtship, if you could call it that.

It had taken another few weeks before they'd made love and she'd been the one to push for it. At that time they'd both been virgins, something about him that had surprised her.

She looked at a photo of him running along a beach on the east coast of the island. She remembered that day clearly. They'd gone driving and parked the car and walked along the beach. The rain has started to fall, the beach was bare and they'd stripped and made love with the rain falling gently around them.

It had been crazy, exciting, passionate, sandy love-making. He'd made love to her with a desperation she could not understand. Two months later, their relation-ship had ended. Another month later, she was preg-nant. Though they'd made love after that day, she knew, beyond a shadow of doubt, Gregory had been conceived that night.

That night, at home, she'd felt the first stirring of life. Impossible, people would say, but she'd known.

She closed the album, feeling the unexpected tears.

Those memories were part of the fantasy world she lived in as a teenager and in her early twenties.

Those days were long gone. The day she'd real-ized she was pregnant was the day she'd grown up and stepped into the real world. No fanciful romance for her—that had been confirmed when George had told her she was no longer part of his future.

The next day at work George called one of his col-leagues into his office. While his chat with Rachel had been promising, he needed to make sure that things were in place in case he had problems.

Although he didn't want to share his personal busi-ness, he trusted Brian Marshall enough to talk to him.

"You have a what?"

"A son. That's what I said the first time."

"Okay, okay, I know, but a son? I didn't know you had kids."

"I didn't either, but now I know. What I want is for you to take care of the paperwork for me. I want joint custody. I'm just getting the information ready, but I'm not going to do anything about it until I see what's going to happen. For now things are pleasant, but you know how women are."

"I know. Remember, I'm paying alimony."

"I forgot. How are the boys doing?"

"They are doing fine. Their mother is doing better than I am. She's not working and getting a full salary."

"I'm sorry to hear that."

"She has been pretty good about the boys and visitation. I get them all weekend. They're adjusting, so it's definitely workable. However, I believe you need to do things the right way. I'll start drawing up the forms and you'll just need to put in the important information."

"Okay, but I still want you to hold off a bit."

"Okay, you're a lawyer too, so you must know what you're doing. Just know that your suggestion is in dispute. I've known too many people who make the mistake of not protecting themselves and then have to deal with serious consequences. If you were my lawyer, what would you do?"

George thought about it. It was true, he would have advised a client to proceed.

"Okay, give me a week and then you can go ahead."

"Good—that sounds better. If I don't hear anything from you, I'll go ahead and file them. I'll send the forms down and you can fill them out and leave them on my desk before you leave work."

"Thanks. I'm glad for the advice."

"What are friends for?"

When Brian walked out of his office, it took a while for him to reassure himself that he was doing the sensible thing. But he was dealing with Rachel.

The same Rachel who'd left without letting him know about his child.

He glanced at his watch and realized it was almost seven o'clock. He needed to head to the gym and then he'd finish his preparation for the trial at home. The gym was the perfect place to stop his obsessing about his situation.

On his way home from the gym, George dialed Shayne's number and waited for him to answer.

"Yes, George. What can I do for you?"

"I need to talk to you about something important."

"George, it's after eleven o'clock. Carla and the kids are sleeping."

"I'm sorry, Shayne. It's really, really important."

"Okay, I'll be downstairs on the patio." The call disconnected.

When he pulled into the driveway ten minutes later, a single light illuminated the patio. Shayne stood there.

Parking the car next to Shayne's SUV, he alighted and walked toward his friend.

He wasn't even sure why he was here.

He sat immediately, waiting for Shayne to sit.

"So what's going on, bro?"

He wasn't sure where to begin but then decided to get straight to the point.

"I have a son."

Shayne jumped up. "You have a what?"

"Son."

"How the hell did you get a son? You knew about this?"

"No, just found out a few days ago."

Shayne paused as if thinking.

"Who's his mother? Rachel?"

"Yes. He's twelve years old."

"Twelve years?" he said, nodding. "Is that why she left?"

"Yes. And didn't say a word. She could have told me."

"She could have, but you did make quite clear the path you wanted your life to take."

"I don't care about that. She should have told me."

"I beg to differ, but then you've never wanted to take responsibility for your part in this."

"My responsibility?"

"Yes, your responsibility. You dumped the girl. You seduced her, made her your girl and then dumped her when you felt she was a burden."

George didn't know what to say. To say he was shocked was an understatement.

"I'm sorry to be harsh, but I'm really tired of you blaming Rachel for what happened. I'm not saying that it was right not to tell you, but I don't think it was wrong based on the circumstances. What did you expect her do? Run back to you and beg even more? In her position, I would have done the same thing."

George stood. He wasn't sure what to say. Shayne's words hurt, but he knew why they hurt. They were the truth. He'd justified what he had done over the years by blaming her for running away and denying that the whole cycle would not have started if he had not ended the relationship.

He walked to the left side of the patio and looked into the darkness, seeing only the blurred silhouette of trees in the distance.

Slowly he turned, walking back to stand next to Shayne.

"Thanks, Shayne. I probably needed to hear that. I remember telling Rachel years ago that I'd be willing to change if she went out with me. You've made me realize something. I haven't changed much in thirteen years. I'm still an arrogant son of a bitch."

"God, George, you can't compare yourself with the man you were years ago. Yes, you're still arrogant and think you're the sexiest man in the gym. But there are good things about you. Good traits each of us has, has always had. Maybe that's why we're still good friends. But it doesn't mean we can't see the flaws in each other and do something about it."

"I think I've really messed up with Rachel."

"Maybe, maybe not. Maybe she still loves you. How do you feel about her?"

"I know I still love her. I don't know if it's like it was before. It feels different. Like I'm not that boy anymore, but still him."

"A bit profound, but I think I understand what you mean."

"I know I'm still attracted to her. I still want her. Is this what being in love is like? You must know. You and Carla, Troy and Sandra. I look at you all when you're together and it's like… I don't know how to explain it."

"Then open yourself to the possibilities. You don't know what's in store for you and Rachel. Maybe the two of you needed the time away from each other. You're now mature enough to appreciate what true love is."

"Boy, I can see what love and marriage have done to you. You sound like you could write a romance novel."

"Maybe. I know I love Carla, and it's not because she's beautiful or intelligent or witty. I just know right here," he said pressing his right hand against his heart.

George moved closer to his friend and touched him on the shoulder.

"You know I couldn't want better friends than you and Troy. The three of us have always been good friends."

"I know, bro. Both of you helped me when my parents died and I had to deal with being a brother, father and mother to Russell and Tamara."

"You know what, Shayne? I know I want that forever with Rachel. I'm just going to have to work hard to win her trust and love again."

Minutes later, as he drove onto the street, the burden weighing him down had lifted. A calmness had settled over him—not the calmness he enforced, but one that came from a sense of expectancy.

Tonight would be the first night since that day he'd seen Rachel in the courthouse that he would have a good night's sleep.

At home George searched in his mother's room for the box of photos he'd found when he'd sold the house and her things. He carried the box to his room, spreading more than three hundred photos on the bed. These photos represented his life and he looked at them with critical eyes.

One of the things he noticed was that he laughed a

lot. Of all of his friends, he was the least serious, the most fun-loving.

He'd always been the one to cheer his friends up when they were in the dumps.

He remembered clearly the night Shayne had received the call about his parents' accident. George had rushed over to the plantation house, and he and Troy had tried to help his best friend through that heartbreaking period. The Knight Plantation had always been like a second home and they had spent many weekends and summer holidays there. Shayne's parents' death had hurt him a lot, but he'd known at the time that Shayne would need his support even more.

One day, Shayne had been a teenager without a care in the world. The next day, he'd become the guardian for his younger brother and sister.

Shayne had immediately dropped out of university and taken over the running of the plantation and the household. He'd been a good father to his siblings.

Photos of George's teen years brought back memories. A photo of Rachel, her short afro, her unexpected smile transforming her into the person he had known... and loved.

When he'd first met her, he wondered if she ever smiled, but then he had discovered her wry sense of humor.

He planned on making things up to her. He would die doing it.

An ache sharper than any he'd experienced gripped him and his desire to know his son was even stronger. He hated having to wait, but he respected Rachel's wishes. Her assessment of the situation was correct and he knew waiting to let Gregory know was for the better.

He had to take his time, let his son get accustomed to him. He didn't want to rush and ruin things. If he did, he could lose his son even before he gained him.

Across the island, Rachel was troubled by her own conflicting emotions. Although her talk with George had gone well, she wasn't sure if she trusted him. The situation between them was too fragile, too potentially volatile, but for now she hoped he'd do the right thing. Her only concern in this situation was Gregory and how discovering who his father was would affect him.

The decisions she'd made long ago were now back to bite her in the ass, and already it was painful.

She walked down the hallway. Gregory would be asleep. Years ago, she'd go into his room and sit next to his bed and watch him while he slept. She'd been amazed at how precious he was, especially when she'd almost lost him in childbirth. Her labor had not been easy and eventually she'd had a cesarean delivery.

Her visits to his room at night had lessened over the years, but on occasion she would find herself entering his room, watching him as he slept and thanking God for him.

When she reached his bedroom, she eased the door open and stepped inside. The white rays of the full moon allowed her to see his face, so much like George's.

Love, big and powerful, swelled inside her. She loved Gregory like she loved nothing else.

She just hoped that George wouldn't want to take him from her.

Chapter 12

When Rachel walked into the kitchen, Gregory was eating a sandwich made with about five slices of bread.

"Mom, I told Gregory not to eat. He's going to want hot dogs and popcorn at the cinema and we'll probably be going for pizza afterward."

"Rachel, he's a growing boy. He needs to eat. You see how active he is. When you were his age you had a healthy appetite too. My grocery bill was high."

Gregory laughed. "See, Mom. I'm a growing boy." He gobbled the last of the sandwich, stood and flexed his biceps.

"You go get your shoes. George should soon be here."

"Why are we going out with him anyway?" he said, pouting.

She hadn't expected the question, but, thinking quickly, she replied, "I've told you already. We went to school together. I'm trying to make contact with my friends. He was my best friend at school. You told me you were all right with us hanging out together."

"Okay," he replied, looking at her suspiciously. He turned and left the room.

"You have your work cut out for you," Grace observed. "He's at the age when any man will be a threat to his relationship with you. Give him time."

"I know. I need time too. I'm trying to take things one day at a time. I'm not sure how much I can trust George."

"Rachel, you know George. You loved him once. Stop imagining what he could be and think of the man you knew. He may be older, more mature, but inside he's the same man you knew. And from what I know he was a good person. I don't know what he was battling with when he called off your engagement, but maybe it was for the better. You're both older now. You should be able to deal with a relationship better."

Before Rachel could respond, the doorbell rang.

There was the sound of footsteps racing down the hallway and toward the door.

Rachel smiled at her mother, counted to ten and walked out of the kitchen.

There was no turning back.

George pressed the doorbell and stood waiting for a response. He'd told Rachel six o'clock, so he knew she'd be ready. His heart was beating fast. He couldn't believe a whole week had passed since he'd kissed her right here on the patio.

The door flew open and his son stood there, eyeing him with a bored curiosity.

George didn't usually find himself at a loss for words, but that was his current experience.

"Hi," his son said.

"Hi," he replied.

"My mom's soon going to be here. She's ready. She was just waiting until I ate my sandwich, brushed my teeth and put my shoes on."

"Cool. I hope you like the movie we're going to see," he said. He noticed Rachel walking down the hallway. *Damn, she's beautiful,* he thought. He felt his body stir with excitement.

"I'm sure I will. I've wanted to see the latest Harry Potter movie for ages. I'll go and let Mom know you're here."

"I'm here, honey," Rachel said, coming to stand behind him. "I'm ready to go when you are," she said to George.

"Good, let's go. We still have forty-five minutes to get there. I just want to be there in time to go to the concession stand so we can get my hot dogs and popcorn."

"Oh, goodie," Gregory said.

Rachel groaned. "You can't be hungry already. You just ate a humongous sandwich."

George watched as his son slipped out the door, chuckling as he did. He waited until Rachel exited the house and closed the door behind her. The whiff of her delicate perfume tickled his nostrils. *She smelled good!* He didn't like what she was doing to his libido.

A few minutes later they were driving along the ABC Highway. It was a Saturday evening so the traffic was light. Thanks to Gregory, who kept up a lively chatter, the discomfort he had been experiencing slowly dissipated. Yet he was strongly aware of the woman sitting next to him.

She seemed calm, but on occasion, when he shifted gears, his hand touched her leg and he noticed the slight stiffening of her body.

When they arrived at the Olympus Multiplex Cinema, Gregory immediately saw one of his friends. On return from greeting them he said, "Dominic and his family are going to watch the same movie. Can we sit with them?"

"Sure," Rachel and George said simultaneously. Rachel glanced across at George, a slight scowl on her face.

He realized what he'd done. He would apologize later, but already he was feeling the fatherly instinct. For a while he needed to put it under control. He'd promised Rachel he would give Gregory time to adjust to his being around. He suspected it wouldn't be easy. The boy was suspicious of him and protective of his mother.

At the concession stand, Gregory requested his two hot dogs and a large bag of popcorn, raising his brow when George ordered the same thing for himself.

For the next two hours they sat enchanted and thrilled by the magic of Harry Potter.

After the movie ended, Gregory asked if Dominic could go with them to Chefette.

"Of course," George replied before Rachel could respond. "I'll check to make sure it's fine with his parents."

Dominic's parents consented, but he could tell that Rachel wasn't totally happy with that. It meant that while the boys were occupied with each other, she would be forced to chat with him.

Good. There were lots of questions he wanted to ask her about Gregory, things he wanted to learn.

When they reached the restaurant, the boys rushed out of the car. He couldn't believe they were still hungry. They'd settled on pizza and he gave them the money to purchase one, along with additional drinks for him and Rachel.

Inside, he led her to an empty table for two. "Let's give the boys their privacy," he said. "They can sit over there." He pointed at a table across from them.

She just nodded, surprising him with her easy compliance.

She sat opposite him, daintily, he suspected in hope that the physical contact would be minimal.

She remained quiet, her eyes focused on where the boys stood waiting in the pickup line. The pizza would take about twenty minutes, so he planned on using it wisely.

"When was he born, Rachel?" he asked.

"February 25, he's almost thirteen," she replied. "He was a very healthy seven pounds, four ounces."

"I want information about my son, but it doesn't mean you have to rattle off all these facts for me."

"I'm sorry," she replied. "I am still sensitive about this situation."

"Just tell me about him," he said. "Please." He didn't want to beg, but he wanted to hear about his son.

She didn't realize how much her not telling him had hurt. He'd missed so much of Gregory's life. Days she could never give him back.

"He was a good baby." Her voice was whimsical.

"Always content as long as I fed him. He hardly cried. I'd feed him and put him down next to me and he'd play by himself and whenever I looked in on him, he would smile at me and go back to sleep. He took his first step when he was nine months."

"Mom," Gregory interrupted. "Here are your drinks. You're sure you don't want any pizza?"

"Yes, we're sure," Rachel replied.

"But we can't eat it all," Dominic said.

"Oh, yes, we can," Gregory interrupted.

George couldn't help but laugh.

He watched as the boys headed to their table, his son strutting with arrogant confidence.

Damn, the boy was so much like him…even his walk.

"You can't deny he's your son, can you?" she commented.

"Nope. I knew from the first time I saw him. If I were to show you a photo of me at that age, you'd think it was Gregory. I'm sorry I wasn't there with you. It must have been difficult being alone."

She did not respond at first, just continued to stare at him.

"Edward was there," she said. Her words cut deep, but that was the reality. He had not been there and he only had himself to blame. He'd been the one to push her away.

"I'm sorry, I shouldn't have said that," she said, her face red with embarrassment.

"But it's true. I wish I could change a lot of things I did back then. I can only try to rectify them now. I promise you that you won't regret coming back home and letting me be a part of Gregory's life. You could have remained in Anguilla, but you came back, knowing that someday I would find out. We're both lawyers, your mother and I are friends, so it would have been inevitable."

He could tell she was at a loss for words, but he had meant each word.

"I don't have a problem with that. He is at that age when a boy needs his father. He's somewhat curious about you now, but I can see he's softening a bit. At least he doesn't look like he'll growl at you anymore."

George looked across at where Gregory sat with his friend. The pizza box was already empty. He smiled. Dominic seemed to have done just fine keeping up with his son.

At the same time Gregory looked over and saw him. For a moment they stared at each other, and then Gregory smiled and nearly broke his heart.

The rest of the night seemed brighter, happier. When they were driving Dominic home, the boys sang a repertoire of local and international hits. He joined in, not realizing that he knew the words to some of the songs.

He dropped Dominic home and then headed east along the ABC Highway. Gregory had fallen asleep and Rachel sat with her head against the seat, her eyes closed.

"You're all right?" he asked.

"I'm tired," she responded, her voice strained.

"Pain?" he asked.

"A little, but nothing my medication won't help. We'll soon be home. I'll survive."

She rested her head back again, closing her eyes. Even in her discomfort, she was still the most beautiful woman he knew. He'd been crazy to let her go. He knew that now. This time he would do it right. He had to gain her trust again and then he'd show her how much he loved her.

He turned into their cul-de-sac and pulled up in front of the house.

Rachel reached behind, shaking Gregory awake. He woke slowly.

"Are we home?" he asked drowsily.

"Yes, you go on up and take your shower. I'll come tuck you in."

"Mom!"

"Oh, sorry. I didn't know you didn't want George to know you still like to be tucked in."

"It's cool, Gregory," he said. "My mom tucked me in when I was your age. I didn't call it 'being tucked in,' but it was our special time together when I could ask her anything I wanted to."

"Oh, I wasn't bothered about that," he replied, trying to sound nonchalant, but George knew better.

"I'll see you when you come in, Mom. Mr. Simpson, thanks for taking us out and letting my friend Dominic join us."

"No problem, son. I enjoyed the evening. We must do it again."

"Sure," Gregory replied cheerfully as he stepped out of the car and ran inside.

"I'd like to say thanks for the night. He enjoyed himself."

"And didn't you?" George asked. He couldn't keep his eyes off her lips. He wanted to kiss her.

"I should go in now," she said, but she didn't move.

"You should," he replied, leaning toward her.

She turned to look at him.

He moved his lips to hers, touching them gently at first, waiting for her response.

She responded like a flower opening. Her lips parted, allowing him entry. She groaned, exciting him with the sound of pleasure. He hated that they were in the car; he wanted to feel her against him, his body pressed against her softness.

When he deepened the kiss, becoming harder and more demanding, her own response changed as she demanded of him.

And then she pulled away, her breathing labored.

"I have to go," she gushed as she opened the door and stepped out.

She walked quickly, stopping at the door briefly before she opened it and entered.

She did not look back. Instead, the light on the outside went off, leaving him to stare into the darkness.

Rachel closed the door behind her, flicking the light switch off, leaving the patio in darkness. She walked to the window. His car was still there.

Then the engine started and he drove away.

She'd wanted him tonight. She'd wanted him. How could she be so foolish? Hadn't she learned from her past with him? But she had no control over her feelings for George. She had *never* been in control around him. Her love for him had come as naturally as the summer rains. Yes, she'd resisted him for a while, but falling for him had been inevitable.

She had looked beyond the brash, arrogant exterior and discovered the gentle, sensitive man underneath. He had tempted her with his gentle touch and she became his.

She moved away from the window and headed down the hallway. Her son was waiting for her.

Chapter 13

For the next week, George spent most of his free time with Rachel and Gregory. Though Rachel felt more comfortable in his presence, there was still the slight niggling of mistrust. She was slowly falling in love with him again. Not like the last time when she had fallen head over heels in love. This time felt better, more mature, as if they were both dealing with their involvement with a lot more caution.

That did not mean, however, that the fire was not there. In fact, the heat between them continued to intensify. At times, his eyes would caress her with the gentlest of glances; at others, they would smother her with burning flames.

She enjoyed her times with him and Gregory, especially on Sundays, when he would take them to explore the island, allowing her to see the startling changes that had taken place in the years she'd been away.

Frequently, her nights would end with them watching a movie—like tonight—or talking about their cases. Tonight was the end of her last week at home. Tomorrow she would be returning to work, an event she was looking forward to. The weeks of inactivity were driving her crazy.

She'd just sent Gregory up to bed as the final credits of her all-time favorite movie, *The Lion King,* scrolled up the screen. He had not wanted to go, despite his drooping eyes. His attachment to George was scary. She realized that she was slowly losing a part of him to his father. She knew that soon she would tell Gregory the truth, something she welcomed despite her reservations.

"Would you like something to drink?" she asked George. "A soda? A beer? Tea?"

"Water would be fine," George replied.

"I just need to go up to check on Mom and Gregory first. In fact, the kitchen is just down that corridor. Second door on the left."

"I'll get it. Do you want something to drink too?" he asked as she walked in the opposite direction.

"I'm fine. I'll make tea for myself when I came back down."

George watched as she walked down the corridor before he headed to the kitchen.

The kitchen was definitely a woman's world. Unlike the rest of the house, the kitchen had been decorated in a dark pink. Not his color, or the kind of color he associated with Rachel, but then he remembered that the house was her mother's and Grace was definitely the frilly, feminine type.

He found several bottles of water but decided to settle for tea too. After a brief search, he found an electric kettle, filled it with water and turned it on.

By the time Rachel walked into the kitchen ten minutes later, her tea was steeping and he was almost done with his first cup. A hot cup of Earl Grey was a lot more appealing than water.

"You settled for tea?" she asked.

"Yes, didn't know you would have Earl Grey. That's the only tea I drink."

"Never saw you as a tea person," she teased.

"I do have a preference for Blue Mountain coffee, but it's pretty expensive here. I only drink it on very rare occasions. Earl Grey is a reasonable substitute."

"I put coffee to rest after my studying days were over. I had become too addicted so I decided it would be for the better." She paused. "You want to go back into the living room or stay here?"

"Here is fine," he responded, indicating the stool next to him.

There was an awkward silence. She remained standing.

The tension in the room cracked like logs in a fireplace.

"Come and sit next to me," he insisted.

She hesitated briefly but then sat on the stool opposite, her posture erect.

"What are you scared about, Rachel?" he asked, his voice low and husky.

"I'm not sc-scared of you," she replied, her voice belying her bravado.

He chuckled in response. "I'm glad to know that. Just wondering why your hands are shaking."

She looked down at her hands. "Remember, I was in an accident. My body hasn't totally recovered."

His expression told her he didn't quite believe that either.

He glanced down at his watch. It was almost eleven. He needed to get home. He wanted to go into the office early.

"I think it's about time I go. I really enjoyed the evening."

"I'm glad you did."

He stood, then turned to go.

"George," she said.

He stopped and turned around. "Yes," he replied.

"I'm going to talk to Gregory tomorrow."

Joy surged inside. He could not wait to be a real father to Gregory.

"Thanks," he said finally. "I don't know what to say."

"Let's hope that he's ready for this. He likes you, so that's a good start."

"I like him too," he replied. "He's a good boy."

"Yes, he is."

"I promise you I won't hurt him," he said. His hand touched her cheek tenderly. His heart raced.

"Like you did with…" She stopped abruptly.

"Like I did with you," he responded softly. "I know I hurt you, Rachel. I promise you, it won't happen again."

She looked up at him, her eyes moist. "I don't know if I can trust you."

"You can," he said, reaching for her. "You can."

He pulled her into his arms but felt her tension. She was stiff and unyielding, but he did not let go. Slowly, her body relaxed against him.

His raised his hand to stroke her hair gently.

When she looked up at him again, he bent his head, touching his lips to hers. The kiss was gentle, tentative in exploration, until she groaned with her need.

He deepened the kiss, wanting to taste her sweetness. A soft moan escaped her lips and the music he heard in his head was the soft tinkle of the steel drums.

His heartbeat raced, beating firmly and powerfully against his chest.

He rubbed himself against her, aching to feel her naked against him.

"Please, I want you to make love to me." Her request, sudden and unexpected, surprised him.

He wanted her, but he did not want this to be only about the moment.

"If we do this, it can't just be tonight," he said, emphatically. "I want you, but tonight will not be enough. Tonight will never be enough."

At first she did not respond, but then the words seemed to drag from deep inside. "No, tonight will not be enough. Make love to me," she pleaded.

"Your mother and Gregory," he cautioned.

"My bedroom is on the other side of the house. It'll be okay."

When he lifted her off the ground, she wrapped her arms around his neck, giggling like a happy schoolgirl.

"Lead the way," he said, loving the feel of her in his arms. His erection was hard and painful. He wished he were at his home. He'd take her right there on the floor, hard and fast.

He followed the corridor in the direction she pointed and stopped when she indicated a door with a Do Not Enter sign.

"Do I have your permission?" he teased, setting her down tenderly.

"Have you ever needed permission before?" she asked, playing along with him. The memories from their teenage years of lovemaking came racing back.

He pushed open the door, let her inside and then followed.

He closed the door behind him, searched briefly for the switch before he found it and turned the light on. The room exploded in a flash of brightness, startling his vision.

He pressed her against the wall, his body hot with his need for her. Her hand eased between their bodies. When she gripped his throbbing erection and squeezed it firmly through his pants, he groaned with pleasure, his penis jerking in response to her touch.

Drawing her to him, he raised her arms above her and pulled her shirt up and over her head. His eyes lingered on her breasts. They were different, fuller but the same smooth, creamy texture.

Instinctively, her hand moved to cover herself.

His hand reached out and stopped her. "Don't," he said. "Don't hide how beautiful you are."

He lowered his head to her. His tongue parted her lips, wanting to taste her again. Their tongues touched and he suckled deeply.

When she rubbed her body wantonly against him, liquid fire surged through him, his knees almost buckling with his need.

George felt her hand by his groin, her hand fumbling with his belt. Eventually, grinning at her success, she unzipped his jeans, allowing them to fall to the ground. When he stepped out of them, her hand slid under the elastic of his boxers, and they too found their way to the floor. She trailed delicate fingers along the length of his penis, causing him to shudder with the pleasure racing through him.

She walked him over to the bed, placed her hands against his chest and pushed him onto it.

He reached up for her, pulling her to rest against him and he inhaled the sweet, flowery fragrance of her perfume.

He pushed her gently over until he loomed above her, his legs straddling her body.

His lips found hers, and her tongue licked him, sending a shiver of excitement down his spine. He pulled away, the sensation too much to bear. He placed his mouth against the pulsing at her neck, raining soft kisses there and then down to her nose and her eyes.

Beneath him, her hands found his erection. He tensed, groaning as the wave of pleasure took over his body, his excitement mounting.

He struggled to regain control. If he was not careful, he would be done before he had time to pleasure her.

A heated coldness tickled his ears and he tried to stifle his cry of pleasure. When she nipped on the sensitive lobes of his ears, he gripped her back, release too close for comfort.

He could not wait any longer. He kissed her on her nose and rose from the bed, finding the condom in the wallet of his discarded pants.

He returned to the bed, standing uninhibited, and rolled the warm latex onto his penis.

When he was done, he rejoined her on the bed. Her legs instinctively opened, allowing him to position himself between them.

"Please, George, please," she moaned.

He kissed her while he guided his penis to her entrance. Her hands gripped his back, urging him on. He thrust his hips slowly forward, enjoying the feel of her tightness. He'd always loved how she felt in his arms. Her legs widened, giving him even greater access to her feminine core. Passion burned like molten lava.

His body tightened and he stopped his building movement. Instead, he sought one breast, already firm and aroused. He took the dusky nub in his mouth, suckling tenderly, enjoying the way she moaned, her eyes closed. He feasted on one nipple then moved to the other, its warmth filling his mouth with pleasure.

When he had regained control, he raised himself above her again, sliding deep inside her moistness with a powerful stroke. She held him tightly, drawing him deep inside. Her eyes were opened wide, pleasure-filled. Gripping his buttocks, she drew him closer and deeper. She raised her legs, locking her ankles around his hips, as he stroked her slowly and firmly. With every measured thrust, he discovered a new sensation, a new height of awareness, a deeper meaning to the art of lovemaking.

Gradually, he increased his movement, plunging smoothly into her again and again, feeling the knowing tingle of release. The hard thrusting of her body moved him toward the edge and when she screamed in pleasure, he joined her with his own cry of fulfillment.

The sun had already touched the island with its typical morning greeting when Rachel woke the next morning. The imprint on the bed next to her reminded her of what had happened last night and early into the morning hours. Her face heated with the memory. To say she had enjoyed what had transpired would be an understatement. George had made love to her and left her aching for more.

Even now she wanted him. Her feelings scared her. She'd always been unable to resist his charm, and he had been a charmer. But when she'd grown to love him, she'd realized that under that charm was a man who was sensitive and caring but so scared to be himself.

She'd loved him with an intensity that, even now, was worrying. Why? Because she knew that she still loved him.

Where would this all end? Was there any hope that they would find a life together? Last night had hinted at the possibility. They had always been so perfectly compatible. The first time they'd made love had been a humbling experience. Their joining had been more than the physical exploration of their bodies, but a deeper, more profound touching of each other's souls.

That night she'd given herself over to him—body and soul. And in doing so she'd lost a part of herself... to him. She'd removed all of her inhibitions and surrendered completely to him, leaving her vulnerable and... his.

She was still his. All those years in Anguilla she'd fought the memories of him, and in the middle of the night, in the stillness of the night, she'd return to the island, his image vivid, until she would smell the musky, masculine scent of his favorite cologne, and in darkness, she would reach for him, begging to feel that wondrous lovemaking.

But she would wake up in an empty bed and realize

it was no more. The tears would fall for a love, lost and never to be.

Now, she'd been given a second chance. But the fragility of its nature scared her. She no longer believed that love came without challenges. She knew the reality and respected the fickle nature of love.

There was a knock on her door and her mother entered.

"You're all right?" Grace asked, her expression one of knowing.

She knew why her mother was here and expected to be embarrassed but strangely enough she wasn't.

"I'm fine."

Grace walked toward the bed. "Saw George this morning when he left." She laughed. "He was so embarrassed he wasn't sure what to do. Of course, I teased him a little. Told him I heard his shouting from my room. Boy, he almost sank through the floor."

Rachel laughed in response.

Grace sat on the bed. "You're sure you're okay?"

"Yes, Mom."

"I always liked him. Always knew that, if he were my son-in-law, he'd take good care of you. He may be brash and somewhat on the arrogant side, but he's a good man, the kind of man I want for you. When I am gone, I will know you're in good hands."

At her mother's words, tears trickled down her cheeks.

"You make sure you give him another chance. Both of you messed up. You were young then so you're allowed to make mistakes. If you don't do it for yourself, do it for your Gregory."

"I'm scared, Mom," she confessed.

"About what, sweetheart?"

"About losing him again."

"You think God is going to bring you all the way back to Barbados to lose him? I thought I brought you up to trust in God. With all the craziness in this world, you think God's not pleased when two people love each other?"

"You always know how to make me feel better. Thanks, Mom."

"Good. You plan on letting that boy know who his father is?" she grumbled.

"Today," Rachel replied. "I plan on telling him today."

"Good. Boy needs to know his father." She got off the bed. "It's almost seven o'clock. Breakfast is done. You'll just need to warm it up in the microwave. Marjorie and I are going to town. I need to buy a new dress for that church service. That hussy Myrna Belgrave don't hold a candle to my style."

"And that's why you're going to buy a new dress?" Rachel asked.

"Not the complete reason. There's also the new deacon I have my eyes on," she said, her hands resting seductively on her hips.

"Mother!"

"Girl, I may be sixty, but I ain't dead yet. You think you're the only one who needs some loving?"

Before Rachel could respond, Grace escaped, her laughter echoing in the room.

Oh my God, Rachel thought, as she pushed away the image of her mother doing the...

She glanced at the clock on the wall. She needed to get up, take a shower and have some breakfast. It was her first day back at work and she was looking forward to getting back into the swing of things.

She rose from the bed, heading to the shower. Everything looked brighter today. Maybe what her mother had said was true. Maybe this time things would work out and she would finally find her happily ever after.

Late in the morning back in his own bed, George woke to the sound of the neighbor's dogs barking. It was a morning he didn't find at all unpleasant. There was a special kind of familiarity in the energy of their music.

Often they had saved him from being late for work. In fact, he rarely set his alarm anymore, relying on their morning salutation.

He slipped from under the blanket, his naked body startled by the chill of the room.

He walked over to the window, looking out. It was just after sunrise.

In the distance, he could see the gentle hills that skirted the St. George Valley, dense with their rich greenness. He loved it here in the valley.

This is where he wanted to spend the rest of his life. He'd thought he would spend it alone but now, he knew he'd spend it with Rachel and his son.

It was only a matter of time.

Chapter 14

That day, when Rachel entered the imposing, modern structure where her office was located, her mind was focused on the tasks ahead. Hopefully she'd be able to reacclimatize easily and be on track with her current cases, some of which had been deferred by the court to a later date.

She exited the elevator on the fourth floor and walked down the corridor until she reached the door to the prosecutor's office.

She pushed the door and stopped when she noticed that her colleagues were standing there, and her secretary, wearing a broad smile, was holding a gift basket of fruit.

Carlos stepped forward and welcomed her back with an unexpected hug, an action that surprised her since her boss was not known for public displays of affection. She was not surprised when he quickly stepped back, looking as if he'd done something totally out of character.

Amid greetings of "Welcome back" and "Glad you're better" she glanced around her, realizing that in the short space of time since she had joined the staff, she had made friends. She was confident about her ability as a lawyer, but she knew that starting a new job in her late thirties would not be easy. Having the acceptance of her colleagues made her feel as if she were really part of the group.

Briefly, she thanked them for their kindness and show of concern and watched as they returned to their respective workspaces.

Later that morning she was browsing through her towering paperwork when there was a knock at her door.

Michelle, one of the junior prosecutors, entered.

"It's good to have you back, Rachel," she said, avoiding looking Rachel directly in the face.

"I don't want you to think I'm being presumptuous, but a friend who works in the administrative department gave me a call a short while ago. I'm not sure I should tell you this, but there were some papers filed a few days ago that I think you should know about."

"Papers?" she asked.

"Custody papers."

No. He wouldn't!

"George Simpson is seeking joint custody of Gregory."

She couldn't believe he'd done this! She tried to remain calm, but she felt like screaming.

Instead, she looked up at Michelle and said stoically,

"Thanks for letting me know. I know I can depend on you to keep this quiet."

"Of course, Rachel," she replied, a finger to her lips. "I'm aware of the confidential nature of something like this." She glanced at the photo of Gregory on Rachel's desk. "He is a handsome boy." She smiled sympathetically and left.

Rachel could not believe it. A wave of sadness overcame her and for a while she sat there unable to do anything. To say she was angry was an understatement. She was angry and disappointed. George had betrayed her. He'd smiled in her face despite knowing what he was planning.

He'd made love to her last night with an abandon that had left her feeling needed and wanted. And then he'd turned around and stabbed her in the back.

The pain of his betrayal was a sharp knife, not unlike that one she'd felt the day she was attacked. She bent over her desk in pain.

Eventually, she rose. He would not do this to her again. She'd endured enough hurt at his hands. She would not cower—she would fight him with every fiber of her being.

She would never have denied him the right to his son, but this…this was a travesty.

In the fog of the thoughts she heard the phone ring and returning to the real world, she picked it up.

Her secretary's voice came over the line.

"Rachel, there is a George Simpson on the line."

She paused, anger still ruling.

"Tell him that I'm busy right now and I'll return his call."

She would return his call later, much later. She knew

that she'd have to talk to him inevitably, but she couldn't right now.

She hung the phone up and returned to her work. An hour later, she realized that she could not focus. She packed her bag and left.

Maybe an early evening at home with her son would calm the rage boiling inside.

That evening after work, George suppressed his pride and drove over to Rachel's home. Her car was not in the driveway, but he still knocked on the door.

The door opened abruptly and Grace's head popped out. She glared at him.

"Rachel and Gregory are out," she said, her eyes condemning.

"I wanted to talk with her, but I'll have to come back another time. She won't talk to me."

"Under the circumstances, what do you expect?"

"Okay, I deserve that. I know she found out about the papers filed in court, but I need to explain to her what happened. I didn't mean for this to happen."

Grace hesitated. He could see her anger was dissipating.

"You want to come in?" she said reluctantly. "You had better have a good explanation for what you did."

He walked inside, his face hot with shame.

"You need someone to talk to and you need advice before you mess up your life and Rachel's again. I'm your best bet."

He closed the door behind him and followed her down the hallway and into the sitting room.

She indicated the bright pink sofa and waited until he sat before she took the chair opposite.

"You hurt her again, George. Things were going so well between the two of you."

"I didn't mean to do it."

"I don't understand."

"When I discovered I had a son I was angry. Before I spoke to Rachel, one of my colleagues offered to check stuff out for me. Unfortunately, the papers ended up on our office manager's desk and she thought they had to be filed."

"But why would you make a decision like that without talking to Rachel? That's the same thing you did thirteen years ago. You broke her heart then and now you want to do it again."

"I know, I know. I don't have any excuses for back then, but I was just a boy. I just got scared at what was happening."

"I'm sure if you had discussed it with her, the two of you would have made some compromise. You know her, George. Do you really think Rachel would deny you your son? If you think that, then she can't be the person for you."

He stared her full in the face; the shame he was feeling intensified.

"If she really, really wanted to keep him from you," Grace continued, "she could have stayed in Anguilla."

"That's true," he acknowledged.

He hesitated. What the hell was he going to do?

"So how do I solve this problem?" he finally asked.

"Give her a day or two," Grace suggested. "She's not ready to talk with you now, but she will be."

"I hope so. I've missed nearly thirteen years of my son's life. I don't want to miss much more of it."

"I understand how you feel and I think he should

know. Rachel feels that you need to give her time, but she doesn't credit Gregory with the intelligence she knows he possesses. He's a smart, mature boy and I'm sure he would deal with this situation better than the two of you. Kids have a storehouse of resilience that we don't seem to realize they have."

"I hurt her so many years ago and I'm not sure how to heal it, heal what we had."

"In time, George. You were always one to want instant solutions to your problems. That's why she beats you in court. She's a thinker. She internalizes things before she makes decisions. Always, except when she was with you. You had the ability to make her laugh. She was such a solemn child before she met you. She needed someone like you in her life, someone to make her smile, and you had the ability to do that. That's why when you walked away she was so devastated."

"I have every intention of making her smile again. I agree with you. I'll give her time, a few days. After that, I'm going to come and see her again."

"You know she still loves you?"

"The other night, I thought so," he said, feeling his face warm with the embarrassment. "At the first sign of trouble, she balks on me."

"Clearly there are issues of trust that the two of you need to work through. You both just have to stop being so stubborn. That's the problem."

He nodded, acknowledging that what she said was definitely true.

"I'll do what you say," he said. "But I'm going to talk to her whether she likes it or not."

"I didn't expect anything else. You know what you have to do. You have to fight for what you want."

"I intend to. I've made some mistakes that I can't go back and correct, but I intend to make sure she recognizes that we all belong together."

"Good."

"So I have your blessing?" he asked.

"Did you have a doubt?" she responded coyly.

"No, but the gentlemanly thing demands that I ask."

"Would you have allowed any objections from me to stop you from going after her?"

"No," he responded without hesitation.

"Then you're just the kind of man I want for my daughter."

He stood, waiting until she stood before he took her hands in his.

"I love your daughter and my son," he said. "I plan on making sure that we're a family. I know it isn't going to be easy, but I'm a determined individual."

Grace moved closer to him, drawing George to her. He rested in her embrace. Since his mother's illness, she'd been the only one he could turn to. He'd not done it often in recent years and he regretted it. She'd been his only link to Rachel and when he'd thought Rachel was forever lost to him, he'd broken his tie with Grace, only making the occasional duty call. He missed the warm camaraderie they'd had in those early days.

When she finally released him, she stepped back and looked at him long and hard.

"I trust you to do what is right. Don't let me down."

"I won't," he said.

She led him to the door, rising on her toes to kiss him on his cheek.

"Get home safely."

He smiled and opened the door, closing it behind him and waiting for the click to indicate it had been locked.

He walked slowly down the steps to his car.

A few minutes later he was driving along the highway, his thoughts on Rachel.

Sweet Rachel. He'd loved her so much back then. She'd changed him in way he hadn't expected. She'd accepted the brash, teenage boy and taught him to be a gentleman. It had not been easy since he'd always considered being a gentleman a bit too proper and wimpy, but the first time she'd refused to get out of the car before he alighted, he'd been a bit annoyed. At that time he'd wondered, *What the hell is wrong with her hands?*

But she'd been more stubborn than he was and he'd really not planned on sitting in the parking lot of the cinema for the rest of the night, so he'd relented.

Over time, he'd realized that treating her like a lady had made him feel good. In reciprocation, she'd treated him like a gentleman and he'd reveled in the attention she'd showered on him. His slight insecurities about his height had dissipated and he'd grown in confidence and self-esteem. He'd blossomed under her tender, loving hands…in more ways than one.

The memory of their lovemaking the other night stirred him. He'd been amazed by what had transpired between them. They'd made love twice during the night and he still felt hungry for her.

Over the years, he had indulged and satiated his need for intimacy, but none of those women came close to what Rachel did to him. Maybe that was the reason he had not married. He had no desire to settle for less than what he had with Rachel.

He wanted what they had back then, what he'd caught

a glimpse of the other night. What they'd shared had been more than sex. They'd connected in the very special way only two individuals who loved each other could connect.

He turned into his driveway, slowing the car.

He'd do as her mother said. He'd give her a few days, but when he felt he'd given her enough time, he would be visiting her home again.

Chapter 15

Rachel had not expected a day to pass without George attempting to call her, so when three days passed without any glimpse of him, she almost felt disappointed.

She closed the file on her desk and sighed. She really was fooling herself. Tonight, when she reached home, she would call him. In the past few days her anger had mellowed. She really should have given him the chance to talk, but she'd been too angry.

There was a knock at her door and her response was reflective and habitual. "Come in."

George.

Her heart stopped.

He stood silently, a determined, stubborn look on his face. A flustered Michelle walked in, her frustration evident. She'd never seen Michelle like this.

"I tried to get him to wait, but he refused. Shall I call security?"

"No need to," she responded. "I'll take care of this. Mr. Simpson *won't* be long."

Michelle nodded but did not move as if she didn't want to leave Rachel alone, but she eventually turned and walked away.

George walked forward. "I came here with the intention of being angry and shouting—if that was the only way to get you to talk to me. But that would only make things worse. We need to talk."

"Yes, we do."

"Are you free to go to lunch?"

She glanced at her watch.

"Yes, I can go. Just let me get my bag. Where are we eating?"

He called the name of her favorite restaurant in the city. Just a five-minute walk away made it the perfect place for a lunch.

She rose from her chair and walked around the desk to stand in front of him. "As soon as you're ready."

He stepped back, allowing her to leave first and then followed.

Outside, they walked to The Balcony restaurant, situated in Cave Shepherd, one of the island's most popular department stores.

When they were seated, she looked at him, wondering how he would approach the situation they found themselves in. Before he spoke the waitress came and took their orders. Though she was hungry, she didn't want to spend too much time deciding on it, so she ordered her favorite: mashed potatoes with spicy gravy and a tossed side salad. The hearty salad made of locally grown produce was also one of her favorites.

"I just want to set the record straight. Those papers were not to be filed," he said cautiously.

"So why were they?" she responded calmly, but he could see the fire in her eyes. "I thought we'd come to an understanding and you still went on and made your plans."

"Are you going to let me explain?" he said.

"Explain? Everything seems quite clear to me."

He stood. "We go a long way back, Rachel. I thought you knew me, but for some reason you always think the worst of me. I know that I hurt you those many years ago. I've said I'm sorry but it keeps coming back to that. If we want to be friends, then you have to let it go or my staying here to talk to you makes no sense. What do I do?" he asked firmly.

"Sit, please," she said quickly. She glanced around the restaurant. Eyes were on them.

He lowered himself to the chair.

"I'm sorry," she said. "I'm listening."

When George completed his explanation, Rachel looked directly at him, searching for the truth and finding it in the sincerity of his eyes. For the first time, she realized that he looked sad. He hadn't slept well. She could tell. She didn't know what to say, whether or not she should give him comfort.

"I know I made you angry. I know it's going to be hard for you to trust me, but look at me. I may not be a different man on the outside, but inside I'm different. I'm no longer a boy. I'm a man. I want my son and yes, I was worried that you wouldn't want me to be his father. I had every right to be worried." He paused.

The waitress arrived with their food. The young

woman looked at him coyly. There was interest in her eyes and Rachel felt the sharp pang of jealousy.

"You're all right?" George asked, concern in his face. "All of a sudden you look unwell."

"I'm fine. I must really be hungry. I haven't eaten since breakfast and it's almost two o'clock. I usually eat around midday."

"So what do we do from here?" he asked. "Of course, I'll make sure my colleague stops the papers."

"I'd appreciate that. I know we agreed to wait before we told Gregory, but under the circumstances, he needs to know. I'm not sure how he's going to handle it, but we'll deal with that when we see how he reacts."

"I promise I'll be there to support you."

She glanced at him, looking at him with eyes that saw the man he was. She'd been so silly.

"I'm sorry, George. For all of this. The years you missed with Gregory. If I could go back and change it I would, but I can't. All I can do is make it easier for you to get to know him now. I already know he likes you, so that's half of the problem over."

"I hope so. I don't know what I'd do if he rejected me."

"I'm sure he won't. He's way too devoted to cricket, and with the promise of going with you to a few games on Saturdays, you're a friend for life."

"At least we have something in common, so that'll be a good starting point."

"Yes, that's good." She nodded.

"How would you like to go out with me tomorrow night? Not dinner, just a drive in the countryside."

She hesitated, uncertainty in her eyes.

"And I promise to be on my best behavior," he reassured.

"Sounds like fun," she finally said. "And I'll hold you to that good behavior."

"How about dessert?" he asked when she put her knife and fork down on the empty plate.

"Definitely not. I can't afford to put on weight. I haven't been given the okay for the gym. I need to be careful not to overindulge."

"Never known you to refuse dessert," he remarked.

"Oh, things have definitely changed. I have a kid now so I know what it's like to put on unwanted weight. I'm sure you don't have that problem. Do you go to the gym each day?"

"More or less. Though I prefer not to go on Sunday. I like to get to church. On Saturdays I have cricket so I still get some exercise."

"Church? You were not much for church when you were younger."

"Didn't I tell you that I have changed? I believe that we should respect God, and going to church isn't a bad thing. I refuse to get caught up in the politics going on within the church. I just go, spend some time with Him and then I head back home."

"I'm impressed," she replied. "There is our waitress. I really need to get back to work."

George called the waitress over and gave her a roll of bills. She thanked him, smiled sweetly and left.

"I wanted to say thanks for accepting my invitation to lunch. I know you haven't been too happy with me lately, but I'm glad we were able to get this situation resolved."

"I am too," she said. "Promise me something."

His eyes fixed on her and he nodded.

"Don't hurt him," she continued. "Please. Don't see this as a fad. Only do this if you plan on being in it for the long haul. I don't want my son, our son, to get attached to you and then you walk away. I'll never forgive you if you hurt him."

"I won't, Rachel. I promise I won't."

"Then that's all I need to know."

When she returned to work, she spent the remaining time meeting with one of her colleagues about a case they were working on and visiting the facility's library to research a few items of case law.

Around four o'clock she packed her bag and headed home. She wanted to spend some time with Gregory. They'd go to the park and while she walked, he could race his remote control car with the boys who usually hanged there in the evenings.

Then they'd talk. She experienced a moment of dread but stifled the feeling. Things were going to be all right. Gregory would deal with this situation well. He was her sensible, mature son.

When she arrived home, he was doing his homework. She gave him a hug and kiss.

"You can go take a shower and get dressed."

"Where are we going?" he asked.

"Bring your remote control car," she replied.

"Oh, goodie. We haven't done this in ages."

"I know. I'm sorry. I'm all better now."

"Good, I don't like it much when you are ill," Gregory said, racing to his room.

She walked to her own room to shower and dress.

Downstairs, twenty minutes later, she found Gregory waiting anxiously.

"You're ready?" she asked.

"Of course, Mom. Let's go." He held her hand and dragged her out the door.

"You told your grandmother you're gone?"

"Yes. She said to enjoy ourselves."

Before she could step forward, the door was opened and he was racing down the steps. She laughed. Her son never ceased to make her laugh.

Rachel walked along the hiking trail for the second time before she came to an abrupt stop and flopped down on the bench, breathing deeply but feeling the exhilaration that came from opening her pores. She felt great.

Across the parking lot, on the basketball court, a group of boys maneuvered their remote control cars. Frequent cheering floated across the complex. She hoped Gregory had won a race or two. Not that it mattered whether he won or not. His enjoyment came from taking part in the actual racing.

She glanced at her watch. It was just after six o'clock. The sun was already beginning to set. It was time to go. The time she'd been dreading.

She dialed the number of the cell phone she'd given him for emergencies.

"I'm ready to go, Gregory."

"Aw, Mom. I'm having fun."

"Fifteen minutes more, but don't let me have to call you."

A wave of relief washed over her. She was prolonging the inevitable.

When he finally came, she felt grumpy, but by the time the car reached the south coast, her mood changed.

"Pizza, right?" Gregory asked hopefully.

"Yes, if that's what you want. But we'll go by the boardwalk and eat."

He looked at her curiously.

"Are we having one of those 'I'm growing up' talks?

"Yes, we are, but not about what you think we're going to talk about."

"Nothing about sex?" he asked expectantly.

"Nothing," she confirmed.

"Good. I think I preferred when I thought it was birds and bees."

She laughed and he gave her a boyish giggle.

Half an hour later, sitting on one of the many benches along the two-mile boardwalk, Rachel watched as Gregory devoured his fifth slice. Two slices had been enough for her.

He closed the empty box and looked at her.

"What's wrong, Mom?"

"Nothing's wrong, but I need to talk to you about something important."

"What is it?"

She hesitated. She wasn't even sure what to say. She sent a silent word heavenward.

She breathed in deeply.

"It's about George."

He nodded. "What about him? You plan on marrying him?" he said, a scowl on his face.

"Remember that I told you that Edward was not your real dad?"

"Yes," he replied, his expression pensive and expectant.

"Well, George is your real dad."

"He is?"

"Yes, he is. He didn't know he had a son until he saw you that day when he came to visit your grandmother."

"You mean you never told him?"

"I never told him. But it's difficult to explain."

He placed his hand on hers.

"You can tell me, Mom. I understand these things," he prompted.

"We were engaged to be married, but he decided he wasn't ready to get married and wanted to focus on his studies and becoming a lawyer."

"I can understand that," he said simply.

"Then I got pregnant and decided not to tell him. That's when Edward said he wouldn't mind being your dad and taking care of you."

"That was cool of him. I still think of him as my dad."

"That's fine, honey."

"So George wants to be my dad?"

"I think he would like to, but it's really up to you."

"Does he have other children?"

"No."

"Can I think about it?" he asked.

"Yes, you can think about it. He says the decision is yours."

"Can we go now?" he asked pensively.

"You're going to be okay, buddy?" she asked him.

"Yes, I will be. It still feels strange. Having a dad all of a sudden, but I like him, Mom. He's pretty cool and he's big. The boys are going to envy me."

Rachel exhaled deeply. It had gone better than she'd expected.

"You're ready to go?"

"Yes. Can I tell Jonathan?"

"Sure," she replied. She knew how important it would be for him to tell his best friend.

He was about to say something when he stopped.

"What is it, Gregory?" she asked.

"Do I have to call him 'Dad'?"

"The choice is yours. You can talk to him about that. I'm sure he will understand if you're not ready to call him that yet."

"Okay, I'll talk to him about it. It'll feel strange calling him Dad."

She understood where that question was coming from.

"I know that's what you called Edward, but I'm sure he wouldn't mind you calling your real dad by that name too."

"You're sure?" he asked, his brow furrowed.

"I'm positive," she responded. "Come, let's go," she told him, standing and waiting for him to take the pizza box to the garbage can.

She reached to hold his free hand and he slipped it inside hers.

She glanced down at him and he smiled up at her.

Her son was going to be all right.

George pumped the barbell for ten more reps then rested it on its stand.

He felt good. The workout had helped to release the tension he was feeling. Getting to know his son was consuming his every waking hour.

He took up his towel and headed to the changing room.

Would he be a good father? He knew nothing at all

about being a father. He suspected that it would not be easy. With a newborn baby things would come naturally. He would have a lot more influence on that child. He would be able to mold that child.

With Gregory, it would be different. The boy may have already established his personality, his likes and his dislikes. What right would George have to start making demands on him? What about punishment?

"Lord help me," he pleaded aloud.

There was a sound behind him and he turned around to see one of the gym's regulars. He didn't know the man's name, but they often nodded politely at each other, as they did now.

He reddened with his embarrassment. The man must be thinking he was crazy.

He stripped his clothes off, wrapped a towel around him and headed to the shower.

He wasn't sure how this situation would all end but he planned on doing everything in his power to earn Gregory's trust…and love.

He showered quickly and left the gym. It was after nine o'clock. He wanted to see Rachel and instinctively he drove the car in her direction.

When he was near, he dialed her number on his cell phone.

The phone picked up on the first ring.

"Hello." Her voice was low and husky, as if she'd been sleeping.

"I hope I didn't wake you."

"No, I was here reading," she replied. He smiled. She'd always loved reading before she went to sleep.

"And thinking about you," she said quickly.

"You were?" he responded. "That's nice to know. I'm on my way to your house. May I come over?"

"Sure, but Gregory is asleep."

"I want to see you," he emphasized.

There was silence.

"I want to see you too," she said.

Happiness bubbled inside him. The feeling surprised him. He hadn't ever really been the bubbly kind of person.

"I'll be there in ten. I'll try not to make too much noise and wake the others."

"That's fine. Remember, they're on the other side of the house."

"I remember," he said. "I'll see you in a bit." He disconnected the call.

He couldn't wait to see her. Already, his body was feeling the stirring of arousal. His penis throbbed with anticipation. It took all of his willpower not to break the speed limit. When he arrived, she was standing on the patio, clad in a robe.

He parked quickly and jumped from the car.

On reaching the patio, he stood before her, feeling her own heat and arousal.

He opened his arms and she moved toward him, allowing him to put his arms around her and hold her tight.

She felt good against him, soft and sweet. He held her tightly, not wanting to let her go.

He bent his head to kiss her, at first brushing his lips lightly against hers.

"Come, let's go inside," she suggested, breaking their contact and stepping away for him, her eyes blazing with her desire. "I have something to tell you."

"Can't it wait? We can talk later," he responded, his voice husky with his desire.

"No, I need to tell you now."

He nodded reluctantly.

"I told Gregory that you're his dad."

He didn't know what to say. His love for her, for what she'd done, surged powerful and intense. When he did speak all he could say was "Thank you."

She held his hand, leading him inside.

He browsed the darkened room. He didn't want any surprises, but both Gregory and her mother seemed fast asleep in their beds.

He opened the door of her room and followed her in. With his leg, he pushed the door shut.

He held her hand, taking her with him to the bed.

She raised her hands instinctively, allowing him to slip the tank top off. The pair of shorts followed. When she was standing naked before him, he cupped her breasts, caressing them with a tenderness that drew an animalistic grunt from her.

"Beautiful," he mumbled before he lowered his head and captured one dusky nipple between his teeth.

"What are you doing to me?" she asked in a soft groan.

He lifted his head in response, smiled at her and lowered his head to the other nipple.

He felt her hands against his stomach before she slipped them inside his boxers and gripped him firmly. He gasped when she stroked him, causing his body to jerk.

He placed his hands against her hips to steady himself, drawing her against him until his penis settled at the warm spot between her legs.

He lowered her to the bed. "I'll undress."

He slipped off his shorts, enjoying the feel of her eyes on him and the look of appreciation when his erection sprang from his boxers.

He knew he was big. He'd been well-blessed, but for the briefest of moments, he felt small and vulnerable.

She reached for him, gripping his behind firmly, her intent clear. She closed her mouth on him and he groaned, the hotness of her mouth causing his body to shudder with excitement.

"Don't," he told her. "If you do I'll be done before you know it. I want this time to last for a while. I want to ride you until you beg me to stop."

She moved away reluctantly, a soft pout on her pretty mouth. He lowered himself onto her, loving the feel of her arms around him.

She wrapped her legs around him, her body writhing with pleasure and he knew he could wait no longer. Leaving her briefly, he searched for the protection.

He handed her the condom, standing as she rolled it onto his hardness.

Her task completed, she lay on her back, her legs parted as if eager to welcome him.

When he lowered himself onto her, he slipped smoothly inside her vagina, loving the feel of her warm tightness.

Rachel wrapped her legs around him, allowing him deeper penetration. With every stroke, her womanhood gripped him, the friction stirring pleasure deep inside him. Beneath him, she moved with him, her rhythm matching his in the dance of lovers.

With each stroke, he could feel the heat increasing inside and he knew he was close to release. His body tensed and he allowed himself to flow with the impending power inside him. When his orgasm came, he groaned out loudly, his body shaking and convulsing.

And then she joined him, her own orgasm as intense, her own cry one of pure pleasure. Beneath him, she shuddered as the heat washed over them.

In the aftermath of their passion, his heart full of his love for her, he whispered softly in her ear, "I love you."

There was no response. Rachel's eyes were closed, her breathing steady and soft.

She'd fallen asleep.

Chapter 16

When she woke in the morning, he was gone, but she'd expected it. She hoped her mother had not seen him again. Grace would be planning their nuptials before George could propose.

Nuptials? Is that what she wanted again? The wedding, the happily ever after. Though her marriage to Edward had been fine, it had not been perfect. There had been no romance.

She slipped from between the sheets, stepping onto the cool, tiled floor. Today she had to take her mother to market and Marjorie would take care of the boys. They'd do their homework in the morning and then she'd take them to cricket in the evening. Next week would be her turn.

The phone rang and she reached to answer it. It was Marjorie.

"Hi, Rachel," she said, "I have a serious problem.

Jonathan is not well and I have to take him to the doctor. He keeps throwing up. I'm so sorry about not being able to take care of Gregory."

"It's fine. I'll get things sorted out." She chatted briefly before she hung up the phone.

Now what was she going to do?

Immediately an idea crossed her mind. This was the perfect time to get the two of them together. She'd ask Gregory.

She rushed down the corridor, knocked on her son's door and entered. He was sitting reading.

"It's breakfast already?"

"No, but we have a little problem. Jonathan is not well and his mom has taken him to the doctor."

"Jonathan?"

"Yes, but I'm sure he's going to be all right. His mom promised she would call as soon as she knows what's wrong with him."

"Good."

"You still have to go to cricket, so I'm going to ask your father to take you, if he's not busy."

Anxiety flashed across his face, but when he spoke he was calm.

"That's okay, Mom. I have to start getting accustomed to being with him—that is, if he wants to be with me."

"He does. Think of it this way—if he didn't want you, would he have asked about getting to know you?"

He thought briefly about what she said and then replied, "That means he wants me to be his son. Right?"

"Yes, he definitely does."

"Okay, you can call him. I hope he's not doing anything today."

"He plays cricket on Saturday too."

She picked up the phone in the room and dialed George's number. He answered immediately.

"Hi, George," she said. "I have a bit of a predicament. My next-door neighbor is responsible for taking Gregory and his friend Jonathan to cricket today. Jonathan has taken ill and she has rushed him to the doctor. Are you busy today? Can you take Gregory to cricket? I have to take my mom on her Saturday errands, so if you can it'd be great."

For a moment, he was silent.

"Thanks for thinking of me. I'll be glad to help. Fortunately, I don't have a game this evening. It'll give me some time to spend with him. What time do you want me to pick him up?" he asked. She could hear the excitement in his voice.

"Well, he usually goes over to the neighbors as soon as he's had breakfast and he'll spend the time there until it's time for cricket at one o'clock."

"I could come and pick him up now and he could have breakfast with me. I'll take him to cricket when it's time."

"Thanks, George. I really appreciate it."

"He's my son, Rachel."

"I'll see you in a bit," she said, disconnecting the call.

She turned to Gregory. "He said he's going to come."

Rachel saw the flash of excitement in Gregory's eyes. A sliver of sadness touched her for a moment. She was going to lose a part of her son. The connection between those two had already been formed. They would love each other. She knew it as she knew the sun would rise each morning.

She was happy. Her son needed a father. He needed a man to help him be the man he would eventually become and for her, there was no one better than his father.

"Go get your stuff together. He'll soon be here. He says you can eat breakfast with him."

"I have my things all packed. I had cereal, but I'll still eat breakfast with my dad." He paused as if he'd not realized what he'd said. The look of wonder and realization on his face only confirmed her earlier thoughts. There was no turning back for the three people in this drama being played out.

He glanced at her, noticing that she was staring at him. He looked away, embarrassed that she'd seen his thoughts.

"I'll go get ready so that Grandma and I can leave soon. She has a long, long shopping list," she told him.

He laughed. "You'll have fun. You both love shopping."

"That's right, my boy. That's right. Is there anything you want from the city?"

"Just a few of the books on the list I gave you."

"I have some I have to pick up for myself. And don't sit there reading all morning. George is soon going to be here."

He stood immediately, reaching to take his bag and cricket gear up.

He followed her down the corridor and headed to the living room when she walked into the kitchen. Her mother was there, putting the plates away.

"Marjorie called and said she had to take Jonathan to the doctor."

"She just called from the clinic. The doctor says it's

a slight stomach virus. She's on her way home, but he's going to be knocked out for most of the day with the medication he has to take."

"Gregory will be glad to know that nothing is seriously wrong. When he comes back tonight I'll let him go over to visit. I've asked George to take him to cricket and he's agreed, so we can still go shopping."

There was the sound of the doorbell ringing. He was here.

Gregory's face appeared at the door.

"Mom, he's here."

"Okay, honey." She walked over to him, bending to kiss him on his cheek. He looked as if he was ready to race back to his room.

"It's going to be okay. You'll enjoy yourself. You can call me if you want."

Her brave son, growing into a man, swallowed deeply. "I'm going to be okay, Mom. Bye, Grandma."

"Come give me a kiss, honey," his grandmother said. He raced over to her, hugged her and then walked away.

The doorbell went again.

"Bye, Mom."

If he hadn't seen the car in the garage he'd be wondering if his son had run away and Rachel was out looking for him. The drive over had been nerve-wracking.

He wondered if he should press the doorbell again.

He raised his hand but paused in midair when he thought he heard footsteps. There was some rattling and then the door opened.

His son stood there. He was at a loss for words... again. What should he say?

Gregory solved the problem. "Hi," he said.

"Hi," George echoed, staring into eyes the same color as his. "You're ready?" he asked, stupidly. Gregory had a bag in his hand.

"Yes. Can you take this bag? I'll get my cricket gear."

George took the bag, holding the door open with the other hand when Gregory stepped back inside.

When his son returned, he carried the standard cricket bag for gear. George could see it was heavy. "Want me to take that one and you hold this one?" he asked.

Gregory hesitated but handed the bag over before picking up the smaller one he'd placed on the ground.

George stepped back, letting Gregory walk to the car while he followed. He reached the car and opened the trunk. He placed the bag inside and watched as his son followed suit.

Five minutes later the car was on the highway heading to George's home in St. George.

"What time do you have to get to cricket?" he asked.

"We have to be there by midday. The game starts at one o'clock. We're playing in Queen's Park."

"No problem. I'll make sure you're there on time."

"My best friend can't play today. He went to the doctor. I wonder how he is doing?"

"You want me to call his mother so you can talk to her?"

"If it's okay. I don't have a cell phone."

"You don't?"

"Yes, my mom doesn't think I need one. But she gives me one to use when I go out in case of an emergency."

"That's a good way of thinking. I'm sure your mom will give you your own when it's time."

"Yes, she told me when I'm sixteen. I really won't use it much. I have my iPod and I don't take it to school."

"Is school very strict about that?" George asked.

"Yes, my principal probably has a big box of them in his office," he said, giggling. "Jonathan got his taken away last semester. He didn't get it back until the end of the semester. He didn't even miss it. Just took it to school because everyone else was. I told him that he doesn't have to do those things to prove anything to anyone."

"That's a smart way of thinking about it."

"People say I'm smart. I'm okay, I guess. I want to be a lawyer just like you and Mom."

"Hope you are not doing it just because your mom's a lawyer."

"No, I haven't even told her yet. She says she'll be happy whatever I decide to do. I like acting too, so maybe I'll get to do both when I become a lawyer."

George laughed. "You definitely will." He paused for a moment. "So what kind of music do you like?"

"Lots. I like everything. My favorite is R&B. I like Rihanna too. She's pretty cool. And I love calypso. I like movies and video games and car racing. My mom gave me an iPad for Christmas. And I like reading." He said the last thing with some hesitation.

"That's good. We have a lot in common. I read a lot too. Can't go to bed without reading."

"That's cool. I get teased a lot about it at school, but I don't care much. Jonathan did at first, but since I came back to Barbados, he's been borrowing all my books. Now his mom buys for him, so we share. I read his and he reads mine."

"And of course you like cricket."

"Yeah, I want to play for the West Indies one day."

"A cricket-playing lawyer?"

He laughed in response. "Well, I guess not. Something will have to go, but if I do become a lawyer, I'll still play cricket. Do you play?" he asked.

"Yes, most Saturdays as long as we have a game."

He was about to say something and then stopped.

"What is it?" George asked.

"I play on Saturdays too. Maybe when you don't have a game, you can come to mine...or I can go with you." Gregory asked.

"Of course. I'm enjoying having you with me."

Gregory blushed, his face lighting up with pleasure.

"Can I say something, Gregory?" George asked.

Gregory nodded.

"I'm not too good at this father thing," George continued. "Haven't done it before. But I want to learn. I want more than anything to be your father. I missed close to thirteen years of your life, but I don't plan to miss any more. I just want you to know I'm here for you. You just have to ask."

"I'm glad you're my dad. It felt strange at first when I heard, but I liked you already. You're lots of fun, but you can be serious too. I can tell you're not being nice to me because you like my mom."

"I'm glad to know that. So what do you want for breakfast?"

"Pancakes?"

"My choice exactly."

He'd been so engrossed in his conversation with his son, the distance to home had seemed unusually short. He pulled into his gated community, nodding briefly at the gateman when they passed. When the car pulled up in front of his apartment, he stopped the car.

"Wow, you're rich!" Gregory exclaimed.

"I'm comfortable, but I'm not rich."

"Do you live by yourself?"

"Yes."

"It must be lonely."

"Sometimes, but I'm accustomed to it."

"I could come spend some time with you, if you like."

"I'd like that. As long as your mom doesn't have a problem with it."

"I'm sure she won't mind. She thinks you'll be a good influence on me."

"I'm sure you're good as you are. Won't want you to be too much like me. You already look like I did as a kid."

"I do?"

"Yes. I'll show you the photos when we get in the house."

George opened the door and exited, waiting for Gregory to alight. He followed Gregory up the steps and opened the door for him to enter.

Of course, Gregory's eyes opened wide.

"Your house is huge," Gregory said, dropping the bag down. He stepped farther inside.

"Come, you want to see the house?"

"Sure."

George led his son through the house, of course having to stop at the entertainment room, so the boy could fawn over the electronic equipment. He loved gadgets and realized that his son did too. He was pretty impressed with Gregory's knowledge of technology.

"Let's go have breakfast. It's only a short time before we have to leave to get to the cricket grounds."

Rachel glanced out the windows for the hundredth time. It was just after eight o'clock and she really shouldn't be worried. This was the time Gregory usually arrived home. It was customary for them to go out for pizza or burgers after cricket, so her concern was silly.

She closed the curtains and headed for the kitchen. Maybe a cup of tea would settle her nerves. What was she worried about? What did she expect George to do? Kidnap Gregory and leave the island?

The illogical nature of her thinking made her laugh out loud. She smiled. She had nothing at all to be worried about.

But she realized what it was. She could be at that very moment, losing her son. Most boys connected with their father and she knew Gregory would. Her son, who she'd had to herself for all those years, she now had to share…and she wasn't sure if she liked it.

She knew it was inevitable, but the thought didn't make the situation any more comforting. Even Gregory's relationship with his stepfather had not been a threat. Yet she knew her son was going to adore George. The fact that they both loved cricket with a passion would only make it easier for the two of them to bond.

She heard the sound of a car pulling into the driveway. She turned the kettle off and walked along the corridor to the front door.

The doorbell rang as she reached to unbolt the lock. As soon as she opened the door, Gregory stepped inside.

"Mom, we won the match today! I scored fifty runs.

My first fifty. We went for pizza and burgers afterward to celebrate. I'm going to call Jonathan to tell him…and see how he's doing."

Without waiting for a reply, he raced in the direction of the kitchen.

"Seems as if he had a good time," she observed.

George smiled. "Yes. *We* had a good time. Thanks for asking me to take him. I hope you don't mind if I tag along on Saturdays when I don't have a game."

"I'm sure Marjorie won't mind the occasional break. Neither of us is a cricket fan and the fathers are the ones who are usually there. You can take the two boys with our blessings."

"Yes, but I was still surprised at the number of mothers who were there. There's a girl on Gregory's team and she's quite good. Better than some of the boys."

"Of course, not as talented as your son."

"No, he's good. I can see why he's the opening batsman. He really pulled his weight since Jonathan wasn't there. I heard that he's a good player too."

"Well, with the amount of cricket he and Jonathan play they had better be good."

She turned to him, aware he was standing close to her. She could smell the lingering scent of his cologne. He smelled good, a healthy masculine scent.

"If I didn't have some work to do tomorrow, I'd ask if I could spend the night." He shifted even closer until she could feel the warmth of his breath on her forehead. She forced herself not to look up. He reached for her and she moved willingly into his arms.

She felt the lightest of kisses at the top of her head and she finally looked up.

The desire in his eyes caused her to tremble. He

wanted her. She saw it each time he looked at her. Inside, a soft warmth washed over her. There was a part of her that still wanted to be cautious, but the other part knew that this thing between them was forever.

The stomping of footsteps reached them as their son came down the corridor.

"Gregory, slow down," she shouted, stepping backward. "Your grandmother is already in bed."

Disappointment washed over her at the interruption. She'd wanted his kiss.

Gregory stopped on seeing them standing at the door.

"Dad, you're leaving?" he asked. He stopped his movement forward. He realized what he'd said. Her head shifted to look at George. He'd stopped breathing, the look on his face one of anguish and joy.

The familiar guilt surfaced. She'd deprived him of so many years. She didn't know how she could give those years back.

"Yes, I have to go."

"Can I call you sometime tomorrow?" Gregory asked.

"Of course, you have all my numbers. You can call me anytime."

"Thanks," Gregory replied. "I'm going up to bed. Bye." He turned reluctantly, as if he didn't want to go.

"Night, Mom. Night, Dad," he said and then turned and raced down the corridor.

For a moment they both stood watching their son.

"You did a good job."

"I did?" she asked.

"Yes, you did. He's a fine boy."

There was silence.

"I'm not trying to take him away from you, Rachel. Just share him with me." He had read her mind.

"I'm sorry. He is your son too."

"I don't want it to be just because he's my son. I want to know you're happy about letting me into his life."

"I'm okay with it. He needs a man in his life. He needs you in his life."

"And what about you? Do you need a man in your life? Is there room for me?" he asked.

She raised her head, looking up at him, looking into his eyes.

"Yes, I need you in my life."

He pulled her to him and she pressed herself against him, loving the sense of comfort being with him brought.

"So where do we go from here?" he asked.

"To my bedroom?" she responded.

"That's not what I mean."

"I know, but right now I want you to make love to me. Then we'll talk."

He lifted her easily and she marveled at his strength.

She snuggled her face in his neck, nibbling on his ears as he walked along the hallway.

He kicked her bedroom door in, entering and then closing it with a skilled bump with his behind.

She giggled. This was the George she'd fallen in love with. Back then, he'd been funny and so full of life. He'd changed and she knew she was responsible for that change.

He rested her gently on the bed, standing above her, watching her with a look in his eyes that made him seem vulnerable, as if what was happening between them would change him in some way.

She raised her arms, stretching them out to welcome him. He lowered himself onto her, careful not to press his bulk too heavily on top, but she wasn't worried, she'd always loved him on top of her.

His mouth covered hers and he kissed her with a desperation that surprised her. She returned his ministrations, allowing him full entry. His tongue slipped between her lips, flickering across her upper teeth. Her tongue responded, touching his gently until he suckled on it.

Liquid heat coursed through her body, causing her to shiver.

She felt his hand slip between her legs until it touched her entrance, slipping slowly inside until she almost screamed in delight.

His hand teased her until it reached the sensitive nub and he rubbed a finger across it.

Inside her, red-hot flames ignited, and she spread her legs to give him deeper entry.

When his hand retreated, she was disappointed.

"Please, don't stop," she said. She didn't want the moment to end.

His mouth left hers, his head shifting downward. His lips moved to her breast, where his tongue worked his special magic. He took one nipple between his lips, tugging on it firmly and sending her on the start of her journey to heaven.

He moved to the other breast, giving it the same treatment before he moved slowly downward until he reached the shallowness of her navel. Her vagina moistened in anticipation and when his mouth covered her, she almost screamed her pleasure.

When his tongue slipped inside her, her body tensed and she immediately forced herself to relax.

His mouth found the core of her womanhood, his tongue flickering against it until her body had a mind of its own and she gripped his head with both hands, feeling the pleasure-pain.

Inside the pressure built and she wanted more than he was offering.

"I want you inside me."

He shifted upward, resting himself firmly between her legs, her legs widening even farther.

For a moment his throbbing penis hovered at the entrance, causing her inner muscles to expand and contract.

His hardness pushed against the entrance, slowly inching inside until she could feel every inch of him. She could feel the pulsing and that heightened her pleasure.

She clenched her muscles, his groan exciting her.

And then he started to move his lower body, grinding skillfully, his manhood sliding in and out, causing her to moan in response.

She could feel the full length and thickness of his penis.

When release came, he exploded like a long-dormant volcano, the orgasm almost painful in its pleasure.

Soon afterward, Rachel's own cry of ecstasy joined his and she too gave in to the joy of ultimate fulfillment.

In the morning when Rachel woke, the space beside her was empty. His scent lingered, that earthy smell that was all male.

She heard a noise and turned her head. George was

on the floor, his upper torso rising and falling as he executed perfect abdominal crunches.

She watched him exercise, the hint of moisture glistening on his skin.

When he finally stopped, his breathing deep and labored, he turned his head in her direction, and when he realized she was awake, a broad smile transformed his weary countenance.

He rose slowly from the carpeted floor, his nakedness causing her to gasp.

Would she ever get tired of seeing him au naturel? She didn't think so. His body was magnificent and he knew it.

He reached the bed and stood right before her, seeming oblivious to the effect he was having on her.

"You want to take a shower with me?" he asked, already reaching his hand out.

She tossed off the sheet covering her, feeling a moment of discomfort, but she ignored it. They *had* spent most of the night making love.

In the shower, they made love again. This time a leisurely seduction that left her trembling and ready to sleep again.

After they'd showered, they stretched out naked on the bed.

"It's almost six. I'll soon leave. Don't want your mother to see me sneaking out of your room."

"You know my mother won't have a problem with that."

"I know. She has always liked me."

"Yes, she was really disappointed when we broke up."

"Oh, I was quite aware of how she felt. The call I got

after you left the island left my eyes stinging for a few days."

Rachel laughed.

"So you're ready to talk?" she asked.

"Why don't we just let things go," George replied, "unless there is something you want to say in particular? I'm ready to let bygones be bygones."

"You're sure? I know that you must still be angry at what I did." Her eyes focused on him, as if she were searching for the answer in his face.

"At first I was, but why rehash that same anger? Nothing we say now will change the events of the past few years. I have my son now. That's all that matters."

She grimaced.

"I didn't mean it that way. You matter so much, I don't know if I can articulate myself as I should. I love you, Rachel. I've loved you from the day you walked into the classroom and didn't even notice I was there."

"I did notice."

"Then you must have pretended not to see me."

"I did wonder 'Who is that arrogant, spoiled brat?'"

"Me? Arrogant?"

"Yes, you were. Still are, but in a good way."

"Okay, I can live with that. I think I just call it confident."

"Yeah, confident."

"However, I prefer us not to talk about me and my flaws. I have something important to say."

"I'm listening," she replied.

"You want to marry me?"

"So that's how you plan to propose?"

"I'm not the traditional kind of guy, but I could be," he responded, bending to kneel on the ground.

"So, Rachel, love of my life, will you marry me?"

She hesitated, a smile on her face.

"You do look so adorable down there. Almost humble," she teased.

"Woman, are you going to give me an answer?"

She placed a serious look on her face, scratched her head and then spoke. "I'll marry you—" she paused "—as long as Gregory approves."

"So it's only because of him?"

She looked at him, wondering how he could ask such a question, then realizing she had not told him.

"I love you too. I already married one man for convenience. I have no intention of doing that again."

He reached for her, pulling her to him until her breasts rested again him. She felt safe and wanted.

His hand caressed her hair, his touch comforting.

"I've waited so long to hear you say those words. For years I was angry with you, but that day I saw you in the courtroom, I knew I still loved you."

"I didn't dare hope for this. When I returned home, I knew it would be inevitable for us to come into contact, but I thought you'd hate me."

"I could never hate you. I was angry when you left, but the truth is, I didn't give you much of a choice. Based on the circumstances, you made the best choice for you at the time. But we must thank God for second chances."

"So how long do I have to wait to become Mrs. George Simpson?"

"As soon as we can get things planned. Two weeks?"

"In two weeks? No, George. This time I want a wedding I can remember. Last time, I did it in court."

"Then your wish is my command. I'm sure Sandra

and Carla will be delighted to help you. You still need to meet them. And of course, Tamara can't wait to see you. You'll get all the help you want. And you know, your mother will be there to give her input too."

"Oh my God. I can imagine her now. She's going to leave you broke."

"I doubt that will happen. I can afford to give the woman I'm marrying the wedding she wants."

He placed a finger over her lips when she started to speak. "No more talking for now. Let's seal this with a kiss."

Epilogue

Shayne, sitting next to his wife, Carla, watched as George walked his stunning bride, Rachel, down the aisle. The wedding had been a touching affair, and memories of other weddings he had attended over the years, in this church, stirred the happiness he was feeling.

He'd seen his two best friends, Troy and George, and his younger brother and sister find their soulmates and for that he was grateful.

Carla's hand slipped into his and he knew she was feeling the same powerful emotions.

He'd had a good marriage and every day he knew he loved his wife even more. A little more than thirteen years had passed since he'd been a guest at the newly constructed Hilton hotel. He remembered vividly that warm night—he'd seen this sexy, beautiful woman and immediately he'd known that he wanted her.

A weekend of passion had led to an unexpected pregnancy and the birth of his preemie son, Darius. His life had changed forever.

He sent a prayer upward, acknowledging the part the Almighty had played in giving him that special love.

Love was incredible and the wedding today was testimony of its awesome power.

When the beaming groom and blushing bride reached his pew, George glanced in his direction, his smile stretching even farther across his face.

He nodded, smiling in return, then he turned to Carla, who looked up at him, her hunger blatant and bold. He knew what she was thinking. Tonight they would make love. Of that he was sure.

He squeezed Carla's hand and she smiled coyly at him. A spark flared in the pools of her eyes.

Tonight, he would show his wife that after all these years he still loved her.

George placed his arms around his new wife. She rested against him and the fresh scent of peaches titillated his nose. They had made love in the shower and already he wanted her again.

To the east, the sun peeped over the horizon. It was a new day, a day that held the promise of his happily ever after.

The wedding had been thirteen years late, but he had no plans to dwell on past mistakes—only to look ahead to the future.

Rachel turned in his arms and looked at him. In her eyes he saw the same love that he knew she saw in his.

She loved him, had always loved him, and for that he was grateful.

"I love you," she said, her words echoing his thoughts.

"I love you too." He nuzzled her neck, and she giggled, a sweet girlish sound.

"I think we're going to have another baby," she whispered.

"Already?" he asked. "We've been careful."

"No, I mean tonight. I feel it here," she said, touching her stomach. "I know we made a baby tonight."

"Girl or boy?" he asked.

"It's a girl."

He placed his hand over her, knowing that she spoke the truth. "I'm sure Gregory will be glad to have a sister."

"And you?"

"Do you need to ask? You know it doesn't matter. I'm going to love any child we have."

She looked up at him, tears pooled in her eyes.

He placed his arms around her again and held her tenderly.

In the distance, the sun, its gentle rays now caressing the land, seemed to smile at him.

He smiled back.

He'd found his sunshine again.

* * * * *